Save Our School

Barny, Spag and Clipper are dismayed at learning that their school is to be closed. Together, they decide to try and save the school by making everyone see what a good school it is. They draw up a list of 'Ideas to Save the School', ranging from entertaining the children in a cinema queue and 'promoting' their school, to having a sit-in at the school until somebody promises to keep it open.

However, all the plans seem to go disastrously wrong, often with hilarious results, and the three friends are in a distinctly gloomy mood when their Headmaster announces some news from a very unexpected quarter...

GILLIAN CROSS

Save Our School

Illustrated by Gareth Floyd

A Pied Piper Book
Methuen Children's Books

Also by Gillian Cross
THE RUNAWAY

First published in Great Britain 1981
by Methuen Children's Books Ltd
11 New Fetter Lane, London EC4P 4EE
Reprinted 1982
Text copyright © 1981 Gillian Cross
Illustrations copyright © 1981
Methuen Children's Books Ltd
Printed in Great Britain by
Butler & Tanner Ltd
Frome and London

ISBN 0 416 89800 9

British Library Cataloguing in Publication Data

Cross, Gillian
Save Our School. – (Pied Piper books).
I. Title   II. Series
823'.9'1J   PZ7.C8825/

ISBN 0 416–89800–9

Contents

1 · The Bulldozers are Coming   *page*   7

2 · What a Picture   22

3 · The Essay Competition   37

4 · The Football Match   48

5 · It Pays to Advertise – Or Does It?   59

6 · Clipper Rides in Style   70

7 · Barny's Secret Idea   83

8 · The Extraordinary Mr Reynolds   103

For Jonathan and Elizabeth

1 · The Bulldozers are Coming

Barny lay on his stomach on the concrete yard and peered under the old bed. Then he rolled sideways and looked under a heap of chairs. Where *was* his football?

'Oi! Gobbo!' yelled a voice. He sat up suddenly, banging his head on the bed.

'Ouch! Clipper!' he yelled back. 'You made me jump.'

Clipper peered over the fence, a grin on her dark brown face. 'What're you doing? Sunbathing?'

There was a shuffle and Spag appeared beside her, pale and mournful as usual. 'Had a fit more like,' he said gloomily.

Barny dragged himself up off the concrete and pulled a Dracula grimace at them. 'Ha ha. Very funny. Lost my rotten ball, haven't I?'

'Blind as well,' Clipper said sweetly. She took a step through the big double gates which said,

J. F. GOBBO. SECONDHAND FURNITURE.
HOUSES CLEARED in large white letters.
Bending down, she scooped the ball out of a broken
wheelbarrow. 'Catch!' She booted it at him.

The ball caught Barny square in the stomach,
knocking the wind out of him. 'Goal!' roared
Clipper.

'That's right. Enjoy yourselves,' Spag said
crushingly. 'We'll only be late for school, that's
all.'

'Groan, groan.' Barny tucked the football under

8

his podgy arm and picked up his anorak, pulling it on as he walked towards the gates. 'Lousy old school. I really feel like it this morning, I don't think. Horrible place.' He joined the other two on the pavement, banging the gates after him.

'Well,' grunted Spag as he slouched up the road, 'you haven't got to put up with it much longer, have you? Only till they get the bulldozers in.'

'Bulldozers?' Barny stared at him. 'You're mad, Spaghetti-legs. Ever seen bulldozers in a school?'

Clipper gave him a quick kick on the ankle. 'You know what he's on about. That letter.'

'Letter? What letter?'

'The one we took home last night.' Spag swung a spindly leg half-heartedly at an empty can. 'My dad went on about it half the night. Jabber, jabber, jabber. Like it was the end of the world or something.'

'I don't know what you're – oh.' Barny suddenly remembered. Pushing his hand into his anorak pocket, he felt the long, stiff envelope he'd been given yesterday. He pulled it out. '*That* letter.'

'You forgot? Again?' Spag looked at him disbelievingly. 'You're a disaster, Gobbo.'

'Shurrup.' Barny slid a finger underneath the envelope flap. 'Let's see what it says, then.'

'It's for your mum and dad,' squeaked Clipper. 'You can't – '

'Want to bet?' Barny stuck out his plump stomach obstinately. 'They never read stuff from school. Never take any notice of *anything*. Unless I tell

9

them.' He unfolded the sheet of paper with a flourish and read it aloud as they walked along. 'Education Committee . . . due to the falling birthrate . . . rationalisation of resources . . . rash-*what*?'

'Measles,' said Clipper with a giggle. 'They're going to give us all measles.'

Spag thumped her. 'Shut up, Clipper. You know what it means. Bet *your* mum and dad read it all right. Didn't they tell you?'

'Sure did.' Clipper forced her dancing face into an expression of seriousness, and imitated her father's voice. 'Caroline, child, I've got to tell you. They're going to close your school down because there aren't enough children to fill it.'

'What?' Barny yelped. 'They're closing it? No more school? Never knew grown-ups had so much sense.'

'Your trouble is you've got no brains, Gobbo,' Spag said pityingly. 'Think they'd let us off school? They're going to split us up, aren't they? Send us all to other schools. Dad said you and me and Clipper would probably get sent to King's Road.'

'King's Road?' Barny stopped abruptly in the middle of the pavement. 'They can't send us there. Not that dump.'

Spag blinked at him through his glasses. 'It's not a dump. It's a new school. You've just been moaning about how horrible ours is.'

'But I didn't know they were going to knock it down when I said that!' Barny put his head down and stomped up the road. 'They can't do that. It's *our* school. The best school in town.'

They had just come round the corner opposite it, and he flung an arm out, pointing to the building. 'Look at it. They can't knock that down.'

It was a tall building, with dirty grey walls and small windows. High, spiky railings fenced it in, and more railings ran round the edge of the flat roof, where the Juniors' playground was. The Infants' playground was at ground level and, over the far side of it, was a separate building, small and even dirtier grey, where the toilets were. Clipper looked from the big building to the little one.

''S not *new*,' she said doubtfully. 'Not like King's Road. My dad says King's Road'll be better.'

'Huh!' Barny sniffed. 'All glass and diddy little chairs. Bet they don't even have proper desks in the Juniors.'

Spag wound his long arms round behind his neck in his usual way and stared at the sky. 'Bet they haven't got mice, though,' he said casually.

'And they've got a football pitch,' put in Clipper.

'We've got the park, haven't we?' Barny yelled at them. 'And the playgrounds? They haven't got a playground on the roof.' He looked scornful. 'They've even got toilets *inside*. How cissy can you get?'

'Nice in the snow,' Clipper said.

'You getting soft, Clipper?' Barny lobbed the ball at her, trying to get his own back, but it just bounced off her hard little stomach and rolled away into the middle of the road. 'Look what you did!' He darted out to get it, and found the back of his anorak suddenly seized by a strong hand.

'Barny Gobbo! You know the rules about playing with balls in the street!'

Groan. It was the Head Mister. Eight feet tall and ugly with it. Barny tried to look meek.

'Yes sir. Sorry sir. Just forgot.'

The Headmaster looked cautiously up and down the road, stepped off the pavement and retrieved the ball. 'Well, perhaps I'll take charge of this, then,' he said. 'Until you're sure you won't forget. Think you can have it fixed in your head by the end of today?'

'Yessir.'

'Well, you can come and get it back at twenty to four, then.' He strode off, with the ball tucked under his arm, and Barny pulled a Horror Fiend face at his back.

'Rotten monster,' he muttered. 'Doesn't deserve to have his school saved for him.'

'So who's going to save it?' Spag muttered as they walked through the gate in the railings. 'I told you. The bulldozers – '

'*I'm* going to save it,' Barny said importantly. The idea had just jumped into his head, but he liked it. Yes, he liked it a lot. He'd always known he was a genius. 'Me. B. J. Gobbo. I'm going to save the school.' His round face beamed kindly at Spag and Clipper. 'You can help if you like,' he

said generously. 'We'll make some plans at play-time.'

The Headmaster was at his most boring in Assembly. 'Now, I want you all to take an interest in these competitions. They're set by the *Sunday News*, and there are two of them.'

Barny yawned and folded his arms across his stomach. Hark at the old Head Mister droning on.

'There's an art competition for classes, and an essay competition for individuals. Now we can – '

Competitions! You'd have thought he'd have something better to do, with the bulldozers ready to move in. He should have been organising protests. Making a fuss. Going on hunger strike. Competitions!

The Headmaster flung his arms wide. 'This is your chance,' he intoned, 'to make your mark. To do something for the school.'

Barny suddenly sat up straight and began to listen. Beside him, Clipper gave a sarcastic groan and he dug her in the ribs with his elbow. No sense, that was her trouble. No imagination. He poked her again and she yelped.

'Barny Gobbo and Caroline Young,' the Head-master said wearily, interrupting himself, 'go and stand outside.'

Clipper was furious. 'Look what you did!' she fumed when they were outside in the corridor. 'Promised my dad I'd be good this term. He said he'd buy me a bike if I kept out of trouble.'

'A bike!' Barny snorted scornfully. 'What's a *bike*? I've got an *idea*!'

'Cor, don't strain yourself,' Clipper said sulkily. She went to stare out of the window and wouldn't talk to him any more. Just breathed on the glass and drew patterns with the end of her finger. Barny decided to ignore her. He sat on the bench and thought about his idea.

The Headmaster let them off with a frown when he came out of Assembly and Barny raced back to the classroom without waiting for Clipper. Before everyone else was properly sitting down, he had his hand stuck up in the air.

'Sir! Oooh – sir!'

Mr Fox pushed his metal-rimmed glasses up his nose and sighed loudly. '*Already*, Gobbo? I've told you before that if you want to go to the toilet – '

'Oh sir!' Barny looked injured. ''S not that. I've got an idea.'

'Good Lord! A whole one?' Mr Fox looked startled. 'Be careful you don't do yourself an injury, Gobbo. Come on, then. What is it?'

Barny was almost bouncing with excitement. 'It's these competitions, sir. The class picture and that. We could – we could do Our School. A big picture.'

Mr Fox pursed up his mouth like an old woman. 'It's nice to see you so enthusiastic, Gobbo. But I don't know that that's very – '

'*I* think it's a bee-oo-tiful idea.' That was Soppy Elaine Potter. She'd actually stopped chewing the

15

ends of her plaits for long enough to talk. 'I'd love
to do Our School. We could put in all the teachers
and the children and –'

Barny tried not to groan. After all, it was a good
thing to have someone on his side. Even if it was
Elaine Potter.

'Thank you, Elaine,' Mr Fox said quickly.
Everyone knew she'd go on all day if you didn't
stop her. 'Well, since we seem to be discussing this
competition, perhaps we'd better have the rest of
your ideas.'

Barny turned round and pulled a Frankenstein
face at Spag and Clipper. Just to show them they'd
better be on his side. Or else.

'Our School,' they said together, obediently.

'*I* think it would be nice if we did a Fairies' Ball,'
said Sharon Grove. Everyone groaned and ignored
her. She was even worse than Soppy Elaine Potter.

Now people had got started, the ideas came
higgledy-piggledy.

'What about a football match?'

'The Martians landing!'

'Sir, sir – a hospital.'

Mr Fox started to write them all up on the
board. In the end, the noise got so loud he put his
hands over his ears. 'Now, that will do. We've got
enough ideas to last us till next Christmas. We'd
better vote.'

Barny held his breath. His idea would only work
if – but it was all right. All the people who'd had
ideas voted for their own ideas. All the people who

hadn't been heard just sat and sulked. And when it came to Our School, Barny, Spag and Clipper all stuck up their hands. And so did Elaine. Mr Fox sighed.

'Our School it is, then. We'll probably start on it this afternoon. Now. Take out your Maths books.'

Poor old Foxy, Barny thought. His face looked droopy, as if he was disappointed. He'd probably been fancying something sensational for the competition. Barny smirked to himself. Wait till everyone realised how sensational *this* idea was.

Even Spag and Clipper hadn't realised yet. They leapt on him at playtime. He had gone up to the playground on the roof and was sitting in their special place, behind the chimney stacks.

'Honestly, Gobbo!' Clipper bounced round the corner in a temper. 'What's got into you? Our School! That's some boring idea. I'd just had this great plan for doing a carnival, and – '

'Should have said, shouldn't you?' growled Spag. 'Nobody stopping you, was there?' He sat on a ledge and twisted his long legs together, letting his face fall into its usual gloomy expression. 'Right then, Gobbo. What's it all about?'

Barny beamed at them, his face creased in triumph. 'It's part of my Idea.' He settled himself comfortably. 'Now men – '

Clipper sloshed him. 'Who're you calling men?'

He ignored her. She was all right usually, but she did have these funny turns sometimes. He

17

went straight on. 'We want to save the school, right?'

'We do?' murmured Spag, raising his eyebrows.

'Course we do. It's our school, isn't it? Best school in town isn't it? Well then.' He took a deep breath. 'We've got to show them they can't just shut it down, because it's too good. So we've got to do Our School for the painting competition and Our School for the essay competition.'

'Is that – all?' Spag coughed delicately. 'The whole of your fantastic idea?'

'Course it's not all.' Barny looked insulted. 'That's only the first part. The second part is – we've got to win everything. To show them how good we are.'

'Even the Football Cup?' Clipper said quickly. 'We've got to win the football.'

'Everything,' Barny said importantly. 'That's the first two bits of the Idea.'

'Hang on. We ought to write this down.' Clipper fished in her trouser pockets. She had bits of almost everything in there. After much rummaging, she produced a bit of chewed pencil and half a postcard. Licking the end of the pencil, she wrote THE IDEA at the top, and underlined it.

Spag looked mournfully unconvinced. 'Doesn't sound much use to me. If they're shutting the school because there aren't enough children, what we want is more children.'

'Don't be daft.' Barny bridled. 'How can we get more children? Buy them in Woolworths?'

'Have to wait for a sale,' said Clipper brightly, 'or we shan't be able to afford enough.'

'Oh *Clipper*!'

'All right, all right,' she said soothingly. 'Tell you what. I'll put everything down.' She wrote.

1. Do Our School
2. Win everything
3. Get more children

She looked up. 'Is that all?'

Barny gave an important little cough. 'Actually, I've got a bit more.'

'Genius!' said Spag sarcastically. He was winding his arms behind his neck again. 'Go on then. What now?'

'It's a secret,' Barny said awkwardly. He wasn't sure it would sound so good said out loud. Even though it was an amazing brainwave. 'I'll tell you when the time comes.'

Clipper licked her pencil and wrote again, saying the words as she scribbled them. '4. Gobbo's Secret Idea.'

'Secret? Who's got a secret?' trilled a voice round the corner of the chimney stack. A soggy wet plait-end swung into Clipper's face and she scowled as she stuffed the half postcard into her pocket.

'None of your business.'

Soppy Elaine sniffed. 'You ought to be glad to let me join in. Specially after I stuck up for Gobbo and his idea. If you're not careful, I won't tell you my message.'

'What message?' said Barny.

'I said. Not sure I'm going to tell you.' She flounced and tossed her plaits back over her shoulder.

Slowly, Clipper bunched her hands up into tight little fists and bared her white teeth. Elaine went pale.

'Course, I have told everyone else,' she said faintly. 'So I might as well tell you. It won't make any difference. There's going to be a procession. Because they want to close the school. It's a protest.' She perked up a bit and grinned. '*My* mum and dad are organising it.'

'Must be terrible then,' Clipper said rudely.

Elaine looked fierce. Then she glanced down at Clipper's fists and looked unfierce again. 'Just giving the message, aren't I? No need to get in a huff. Just tell your parents, that's all.' She gave a rather snooty sniff and took herself off in a hurry.

'Procession!' Clipper said in disgust.

Spag unwound his arms and looked at his fingernails. 'An idea doesn't have to be crazy,' he said, 'just because Soppy Mr and Mrs Potter think of it.'

'We don't need their ideas,' Barny said stubbornly. 'Got our own, haven't we? We don't need anything to do with them.' Spag looked as if he might argue, and once he got started on that no one could make any impression. Barny changed the subject quickly. 'It was good the way you got it out of her though, Clipper. You didn't have to lift a finger.'

'A jelly'd fight back as soon as her.' Clipper looked regretful. 'None of the girls in this school are any good fighters. And my mum says I mustn't fight the boys. She says it's not ladylike.'

Thrusting her hands into her trouser pockets, she slouched off mournfully towards the classroom.

2 · What a Picture

When they came in from Dinner Playtime there was a huge sheet of white card, all clean and unmarked, blutacked to the long wall of the classroom. It was headed in Mr Fox's neat, precise print. OUR SCHOOL BY CLASS 2.

'Yum,' said Clipper. 'Oh, yum, yum!'

Mr Fox wagged a finger at her. 'Now, now, Caroline. Afternoon register first. Then I'm going to explain before we do any painting.'

Clipper slumped into her chair and looked longingly at the piece of card. 'Would've been smashing for doing a carnival,' she muttered in a rebellious voice. 'Would've been really good.'

Barny heard what she was saying and frowned at her. She didn't seem to have got into his Idea properly yet. He glanced the other way, at Spag. But there was never any telling with Spag. He just looked like doom, as usual.

Mr Fox finished making his neat marks on the register, snapped it shut and put the top tidily back on his pen. Then he looked up, straight at Spag. 'Think you can draw us a picture of the school, James? Just the buildings? At least *you'll* get the right number of windows.'

Spag shrugged his shoulders, without altering his expression of deep gloom, and took out his pencil.

'Not yet, boy. Not yet,' Mr Fox said twitchily. 'I must organise everyone else first, or there'll be bedlam.'

Spag started to sharpen his pencil to a fine point, making a neat heap of shavings on his desk, while Mr Fox distractedly smoothed his thinning hair.

'I want the rest of you to do separate pieces to cut out and stick on. Children, teachers, that kind of thing. Let me see. Caroline – can you do some children? And –'

On and on he went, doling out the good jobs and the not so good jobs. Barny stared down at his desk and scrawled on the lid with a biro. Bet Foxy wasn't going to choose him for anything good. Even if it was part of his great plan for saving the school. It was always the same in Art. He never got any good things to do. I could be a genius for all they know, he thought darkly to himself. I could be the best painter in the world. They'd never know. All I ever get to do is rotten bits of wall, and trees, and pebbles on the beach, and –

'Railings,' Mr Fox said sharply. 'Gobbo, are you with us, or have you gone away on holiday?'

'Railings, sir?' Barny said.

'Yes. You can paint some railings to be cut out and stuck on the picture.'

Told you so, Barny muttered to his desk. Rotten old railings. Boring old bits of metal. Still, they were part of the school after all. He got up and joined in the general shuffle round and moving of desks that always went on at the beginning of painting. That was usually quite good. It gave you a chance to bump people you didn't like. He actually managed to spill a jar of water down Soppy Elaine's front without anyone realising it was him.

Spag was already at work, ignoring everyone else. He wasn't really any good at Art. Numbers were his thing. But he liked anything he could do with a ruler, and counting windows was right up his street. He was much too busy to speak to anyone. When they'd moved the desks together, Barny wangled himself a place next to Clipper, so that they could chat.

'What're you going to do, Clipper?'

She giggled. 'I'm going to do Sharon Grove and Elaine,' she whispered. 'Playing fairies in the playground.'

Barny pulled a face. '*I'm* doing railings.' Railings suddenly sounded quite sensible after all. He picked a bit of charcoal out of the box and stared at his piece of paper.

Ten minutes later, he was still staring. 'Oi, Clipper,' he whispered.

'Shut up,' Clipper said crossly. She was painting yellow wiggles for Elaine's plaits.

'Clipper!' Barny pointed at his paper. 'I can't do them. They keep coming out like sticks.'

'Railings?' Clipper looked up scornfully. 'Anyone can do railings.'

'But I can't remember what they look like.'

'Oh, you!' Clipper snatched impatiently at his charcoal. 'Look, they're like this. Straight, with a bit across near the top and a twiddle bit right at the very top. There.'

Barny looked at what she had sketched. It looked a bit fat somehow. More like a sausage than a railing. A sausage with one end popped and the sausage-meat bursting out. Still, it was better than what he had drawn. He picked up the charcoal again and bent forward to draw some more.

As he bent over, he bumped something behind him.

'Gobbo!' Spag straightened up and shouted at him. 'You've jogged me. Made my line go all crooked. Can't you keep your body over by the desk?'

'My body is over by the desk,' Barny said with dignity. 'It's just over by you as well. It goes further than the average body.'

'Well, make it go in another direction,' snapped Spag. 'I'm almost ready to start painting.'

'I *am* ready,' Barny said. 'I'm going to paint my railings black.'

He liked the black paint best. When he pushed his brush into it, it oozed over and round in a thick, juicy cream. Better than mud. Like hot, runny tar the road men used. He spent a long time stirring and squishing it about, until Mr Fox prodded him with an irritable finger.

'On the paper, Gobbo. Not all over yourself. We don't want to send you home looking like a sweep.'

'There's not enough paint in the whole room to cover Gobbo's body,' Clipper said cheekily. She was holding her hand over her paper, because she'd just started to draw a picture of Mr Fox.

Mr Fox's mouth almost smiled. Barny ignored them both and started to paint his railings, carefully spreading the thick black paint up between the lines. And not only between the lines. He spread it up his arms and plastered it in blotches on his face. His hands were covered. But he was much too busy to notice. He didn't even notice that Spag, behind him, had started to paint his huge drawing of the school a dirty grey colour. He didn't notice the quick workers coming up with their figures, already painted and cut out, to have them stuck on the card. He was concentrating on spreading the thick black paint.

At last he finished. All the railings were gleaming black. They were a bit fat, though. Didn't they look like a row of *burnt* sausages now? He took a step backwards to get a clearer look at them.

27

'Gobbo!' yelled Spag's voice in his ear. Everyone looked up.

Startled, Barny took another step backwards, staggered, and put out a hand behind to steady himself.

'Gobbo!' Everybody shrieked. Too late. Barny realised what had happened as his bottom bumped something and he felt his sticky, painty hand meet something else sticky and painty.

'Oh, Gobbo.' Mr Fox pursed up his lips and shook his head wearily.

Slowly, Barny peeled himself off the piece of card stuck to the wall and turned round to look at it. In the middle of it was an enormous drawing of the school, painted grey. But there were two places where it wasn't grey now. One was at the top, where three windows were completely blotted out by a big, black handprint, with all the fingers clear. The other was right in the centre. A huge round patch had been rubbed almost bare of paint.

'Coo!' said Elaine with satisfaction. 'Your mum'll go mad when she sees the seat of your trousers.'

Suddenly the class started to laugh. People clutched at each other and stamped their feet on the floor, not taking any notice of Mr Fox's frowns. Barny, feeling his face go red, turned his back on them all.

'Sorry,' he muttered to Spag. 'Didn't mean to spoil your picture.'

''S all right.' Spag stared gloomily at the

damage. 'Suppose I can paint in the middle again. Don't know what to do about the top, though.'

'You could put in a stormcloud,' Barny said helpfully.

Spag just looked at him.

At that moment the bell rang and everyone forgot about Barny in a dash for the door. He let them go and then made for the cloakroom, to get rid of the paint on his hands. Somehow, he didn't feel quite so keen on black paint as he had before.

When his hands were pink again – and the ends of his sleeves were dark grey – he thudded up the stairs towards the playground. He wanted to find Clipper and Spag, so that they could have another talk about his Idea.

But it wasn't any use. Spag was walking round and round the playground, peering through the railings at the view to see if there was anything that he could put in his picture. And Clipper, at first, was nowhere to be found. When she did appear, she wouldn't say where she'd been. Just kept pointing a finger at Barny and going off into gales of giggles. It really was one of her stupid days. Barny was glad when the bell went for the end of playtime.

As its jangling noise sounded across the rooftop, Spag turned round and stopped staring off into the distance. 'Come on then.' He dug Barny in the ribs and almost smiled. Amazingly. 'Let's go and look at the disaster area.'

But it wasn't as easy as that. When they got to the classroom, they couldn't see the picture at all. They couldn't even see the wall. There was a great crowd of children – almost everyone else in the class – pushing, shoving and pointing.

'What's up?' called Spag. But nobody heard him, because of the noise.

Then Elaine spun away from the group. 'Ooh, it's terrible!' There was a delighted grin all over her face. 'Guess what someone's done. There's going to be ever such trouble!'

'Trouble?' Clipper came up behind and peered over Spag's shoulder. 'What trouble?'

'Oh, I couldn't tell,' Elaine giggled again. 'It's too rude.'

Spag shoved her out of the way impatiently and

bellowed at the crowd of backs. 'Get out of the way! I want to see my picture!' They heard him all right that time. Gradually a gap cleared. Barny, Spag and Clipper stared.

'Oh my,' Clipper said softly at last. 'It does look awful, doesn't it?'

'Mr Fox'll go mad,' Spag said. Clipper glanced sideways at him and gave a sudden giggle.

'I don't think it's funny,' Barny said stiffly. He looked back at the picture. Up at the top, where his hand had left its black print, someone had scrawled THE BLACK HAND GANG in enormous, straggling letters. And, lower down, there was an arrow pointing to the big, round bare patch. At the other end of the arrow it said, GOBBO'S BUM WAS HERE.

'Felt pen.' Spag's voice was doom-laden. 'We'll never be able to paint over it.'

'Foxy!' someone yelped from the doorway. With automatic speed, they all leaped to their desks, standing stiffly to attention with blank, innocent faces. Just to show the writing was nothing to do with them.

Slowly and suspiciously, Mr Fox walked into the room. He could tell that something was up. His eyes flickered from face to face, searching, and suddenly came to rest on the picture. For a moment he was quiet, while he took it in. Then he snapped, 'Well? Who was it?'

No one moved or spoke.

'Who was it?' he said more softly, clipping the

words off. 'Who ruined a perfectly good, expensive piece of white card?'

Well, thought Barny. Did he really imagine anyone was going to own up after he'd said that? Must be daft.

'Gobbo,' said Mr Fox.

'No sir.' Barny looked up with a jump. 'Honest. It wasn't me. I didn't –'

'Gobbo,' Mr Fox said patiently, 'I was not accusing you of this piece of vandalism. I was simply asking you to help take that ruined piece of card to the dustbins. And you.' He pointed at Spag. 'And Caroline.'

'And shall we fetch the new piece as well?' Clipper said helpfully.

'New piece? *New piece?*' Mr Fox stared at her, almost stuttering. 'Do you seriously suppose that anyone is going to trust this class with a new piece of card? After what happened to this one? No, you've had your chance. Now get that – that *rubbish* – off to the dustbin, and be quick about it.'

Clipper's eyes widened. Her mouth opened and shut, but nothing came out. Mr Fox looked at her.

'Something you want to say, Caroline?'

'N-no, Mr Fox.'

'Then get on with it.'

Spag peeled the edges of the card carefully off the wall and the three of them picked it up.

'And mind the paint, Gobbo. It's still wet,' Mr Fox said.

Everyone roared with laughter as they man-

32

œuvred the card out of the door. It was not an easy thing to carry. The middle bent first to one side and then to the other whenever Clipper forgot to steady it.

'Stop wiggling, you two,' she hissed as they went off down the corridor.

'Not strong enough to hold it?' said Barny sweetly. He gave the card another wiggle and the damp, painted side bellied out, just as old Mrs Rumbelow came hurrying round the corner.

'Children!' She skipped sideways like a ballet dancer. 'Be careful with that painting.' Then she bent down and peered at it, with a frown. 'If you can call it a painting,' she said sarcastically. 'Take it away at once.'

She tutted off up the corridor, while Barry pulled a face at her back.

'But where are we taking it?' Spag said suddenly.

'Away!' Clipper flourished a hand, and the card wobbled dangerously. 'Far, far away into the misty distances, where never man or old Rumbelow shall find it again, where vast desert spaces –'

'I think,' said Barny, 'she means up by the dustbins.'

'Course I do,' Clipper said. 'Where else? It's too big to go in, but we can prop it up against them.'

Spag sighed noisily. 'Why don't you try looking out of the window?'

They did. It was raining furiously. Spag studied the wet windows with grim interest. 'It'll be a pulp by the time the dustmen come.'

'Not if they come today,' Barny said.

'Friday,' Spag said firmly. 'Three days to go.' It was the kind of thing he always knew. 'So what are we going to do with it?'

'Oh, shove it by the door.' Clipper was bored. 'Mr Pratt'll deal with it when he comes round caretaking.'

There was a long piece of blank wall between the Headmaster's office door and the back door out to the dustbins. Barny nodded at it. 'This'll do.'

'I'll write RUBBISH on it,' Clipper said. 'Just so Mr Pratt knows when he comes round.' They propped the card up against the wall and she pulled out her stubby pencil and started to scratch away. After a moment or two, she began to grin and Barry leaned over her shoulder to see what she was up to. She had written RUBBISH in one of the top corners of the picture and now she was drawing down at the bottom. Barny peered.

'What's that?'

'Oh, Gobbo!' Clipper finished the figure's feet and then drew in two long plaits with their ends in the pencilled mouth. 'Can't you guess?' She wrote 'Soppy Elaine Potter' underneath it in big, untidy letters. 'I just thought I'd make up for not getting my people stuck on.'

'People? Call that a person?' Spag said scornfully. He snatched the pencil out of her hand and began to draw in the empty space next to where she had written RUBBISH. '*This* is a person.' Spag couldn't really draw at all, except when it meant measuring and using a ruler. But they could tell who it was meant to be, because it was half as tall as the school and had a long straggling moustache. Just like the Head Mister. Barny and Clipper started to giggle.

But just at that moment, the door of the Headmaster's office clicked, as if it were about to open. Spag dropped the pencil and the three of them scurried off, down the corridor and round the corner.

Clipper stopped first. 'Spag! You porridge-fingered dumbhead! You left my pencil.'

'That wasn't a pencil. It was half an inch of chewed tree stump.'

'You –'

Clipper looked as though she might hit Spag, so Barny said quickly, 'I'll get it.'

He tiptoed back along the passage, taking huge steps and lifting his feet high in the air. There was no sign of the Head Mister, but three boys from Class One were coming along the corridor, carrying another sheet of white card. Class One's picture.

'Where've we got to put this thing?' one of them said.

'Dunno. Somewhere along here. Oh look,' a second boy pointed, 'there's one here already. Miss said by the Head Mister's office.'

'Some picture!' The three boys crowded round, staring at the card that Barny, Spag and Clipper had left. 'Looks more like a nasty accident.'

Barny nearly bounced out to tell them it was

meant for rubbish. Then he recognised the third boy. Spotty McGrew. He'd fall about if he heard how the picture had been ruined. He'd shout 'Painty bum!' for ever. Barny lurked cautiously around the corner until the three boys had propped up their picture in front of Class Two's.

He went on lurking until they disappeared up the other corridor, and then he darted down and snatched up Clipper's pencil stub. As he ran off again, he heard a voice in the other corridor saying, 'Put your picture by the Head Mister's office. There's a pile. You can't miss it.'

It was a giggle really. Their picture getting mixed up with the proper competition entries. He hurried back to tell Spag and Clipper, but by the time he caught them up they were already in the classroom, and there wasn't a chance.

By the end of school, he'd forgotten all about it. He was too busy working out what he was going to tell his mum about his trousers. He could imagine already how her huge face would go purple with rage. He could hear her ferocious voice bellowing. Perhaps if he said –

But none of that was any use when he got home.

3 · The Essay Competition

Cracking his whip over the children's heads as they cowered in the corner, the wicked Headmaster smiled ferociously and twirled his moustache.

'You will never escape!' he shouted. 'I have put a bomb somewhere in the school.'

Clipper gave a little wriggle of delight. She was writing her story for the essay competition and she was enjoying herself. Her head leaned sideways on her hand and the pink tip of her tongue stuck out between her lips to help her concentrate.

'Mercy! Mercy!' shouted all the children. But it was no use!! The door of the cellar clanged shut and they heard the key turn in the lock. Only brave Arabella had the courage to stand up and shout 'Boo!' to the wicked Headmaster. She –

'Right.' Mr Fox looked at his watch. 'Nearly time for the bell. Put your things away tidily all of you.'

'Oh, sir!' Clipper said reproachfully.

Barny's hand shot up. 'Sir! Sir! Ooh, sir!' he shouted, bouncing up and down in his chair.

'Yes, Gobbo?' Mr Fox looked at him over the top of his glasses. 'Sat on an ants' nest?'

'Oh, *sir*! I just wanted to say, if we haven't finished our work for the competition, can we take it home to do?'

'My goodness me!' Mr Fox said. 'That's the first time I've ever heard you offering to work.'

'I've finished,' said Elaine virtuously. 'I've done twelve pages. All about my holiday in Switzerland.'

'Again?' Spag said. 'Must be the four-hundredth time you've written about it. You were in the Infants when you went.'

Elaine tossed her head. 'I'd have thought you'd be pleased to hear about it. After all, I *am* the only person in this class who's ever been to Switzerland.'

'The way you go on about it –' started Spag.

Mr Fox coughed loudly.

'I know I'm only the teacher in this class, but can *I* say something? Mmm?' He frowned at Spag and Elaine and then looked across at Barny. 'Nice to see you so keen, Gobbo. Makes a pleasant change, I must say. Yes, anyone who wants to can carry on writing at home, but you *must* bring the entries back tomorrow, because that's when we're choosing the one to send from this class. Right?'

Clipper scooped up her pages in a higgledy-piggledy mess. Spag stacked his neatly. Barny only had one piece. He flapped it at the other two.

'Oi! You coming up the yard? After school?'

All three of them met in the Gobbos' yard at four o'clock, waving their pieces of paper. But before they could talk they had to hunt out a den to sit in. They had to find a new den nearly every time, because Barny's dad kept moving the heaps around. Where there'd been a good cave in the junk one day might be just a stack of rusting barbed wire by the next afternoon. And if they didn't search quietly, Mrs Gobbo's massive head would poke out of the kitchen window, and they'd hear her yelling, 'You in them heaps again? Just wait till I get you, you little monsters!'

Today they were lucky. There was a huge old-fashioned bath, the kind with feet, standing like a lifeboat in the middle of everything. Chairs and bits of piping were piled all around, making a sort of fence, and once they'd wriggled in, no one could see them. Clipper and Spag made Barny sit up at the top end of the bath, because of the plughole. 'You're padded better than us,' Clipper said bossily. 'It won't dig into you. And Spag can go in the middle, because he's so good at folding himself up.'

'Thanks a lot,' Spag said grimly. He pulled his knees up to his chin and wrapped his arms around them. Then he looked gloomily from Barny to Clipper and back again, his glasses sliding down his nose. 'Well?'

'Got to read out what we've written so far, haven't we?' Barny said importantly. 'They're only sending one from each class to the competition,

so if we pick the best of ours and all help to finish it, we can make it really good, and – '

'That's just got to be mine,' Clipper said enthusiastically. 'It's the most exciting story you ever heard. It's *tough*. Just wait till you hear.'

She started to read, in a bloodcurdling voice.

My School

'*This is my school,*' *the Headmaster said cruelly to the new children.* '*You have to do what I say, or I will lock you up. Today you are going to build me a swimming pool for myself and –*

Barny coughed, 'You weren't supposed to write a story,' he interrupted. 'You should've written about the history of the school or something. Like I did.'

Clipper sniffed and looked injured.

'*I* gave the facts,' Spag said with pride. 'The measurements, and the number of windows, and the number of desks and – '

Clipper put her hands over her ears. 'It sounds boring. It sounds the most boring thing anyone ever wrote.'

Spag shrugged, resignedly. 'Looks like this whole competition's going to be a disaster, then, doesn't it? Just like the picture one.'

'That awful picture!' Clipper snorted. Spag gave a twisted grin.

'There was one good thing about it,' he said. 'Throwing it away. I enjoyed that.'

41

Suddenly Barny remembered. He opened his mouth to tell them what had happened. But before he could speak, Clipper said forcefully, 'I think we should vow never to mention it again. In fact, I'll punch anyone who does.'

Barny shut his mouth again. Perhaps he wouldn't tell them after all.

'Still,' Spag looked thoughtful, 'I wouldn't mind knowing who wrote those things on the card.'

'Hum.' Clipper turned a richer colour and stared at her grimy plimsolls, propped up on the edge of the bath. 'Actually –'

'Clipper!' said Barny. 'Was it you?'

'Well, I thought Foxy would let us have a new piece of card. So we could do a carnival after all.'

'Huh!' Spag scowled at her. 'A right mess you made of it.'

'It wasn't me,' Clipper said sulkily. 'It was Gobbo. And anyway,' she smiled suddenly, 'I think it was funny. When his bum went splat!'

Slowly, Spag's long face twisted into a smile, and his creaky chuckle oozed out of it. Barny looked hurt.

'But you wouldn't have liked it,' he said with dignity. 'It's only because we've got such rotten small classrooms. It was horrid. Backing away and suddenly going squish – suddenly squishing –'

He could not get any further because, all at once, he saw it. It *was* funny. He began to giggle helplessly.

The three of them bent forwards, roaring with

laughter and punching each other, until Clipper, in her glee, started to drum her feet against the sides of the bath, setting the bits of pipe clanging and rattling.

A gigantic square head poked out of the kitchen window and Mrs Gobbo's enormous voice bellowed at them. 'You in them heaps again, Barny Gobbo?'

They cowered lower in the bath. But when Mrs Gobbo yelled again, her voice was softer. 'I thought you'd all be in here. Just made a cake. Don't you want any?'

'Yum,' said Clipper. 'I need cake to build my muscles. Can't we go and have some? We can come back later and do these essays.'

'Your mum may be loud,' Spag said thoughtfully, 'but she makes delicious cakes. Let's leave all this stuff and have a tea break.'

But Barny beat them both. He was halfway to the kitchen door by the time the two of them had clambered out of the bath. And at the door he met the smells wafting out of the kitchen. Chocolate cake! He leaped through the door. After all, they needed to get their strength up before they did any more writing. Tiring, writing was.

But when they'd eaten all the chocolate cake there were cartoons on television, and after the cartoons it was getting dark, and Spag and Clipper both had to run home quickly before they got into trouble.

Barny woke up quite suddenly in the middle of

43

the night. It was a noise that woke him up. Rain. Not little pitter-patter rain on the windows, but heavy, slooshing rain that slurped along the gutters and gurgled in the drainpipes.

When he realised what was happening, he opened his eyes in the dark and grinned to himself. Serve Dad right for forgetting to put the baths and things upside-down. He hated coming out in the morning and finding them full of water.

He shut his eyes again, ready to go to sleep. But he couldn't. Something was niggling away at the back of his mind where he couldn't catch hold of it.

He rolled over, but he kept getting more and more wide awake. The niggly thing was chasing all round his head. Something to do with rain and baths and – BATHS! He jerked upright, and almost gave a yelp, before he remembered not to wake his parents up. Baths. Of course. He got out of bed and padded to the window, pulling the curtains aside so that he could press his nose against the glass.

But he couldn't really see anything. Only rain and darkness and more rain. For a moment he thought how nice it would be to climb back into his warm, comfortable bed and forget about what was happening outside. Then he remembered that he was B. J. Gobbo, the Saviour of the School, the person with the Idea. Sighing a little, he padded across his bedroom, through the door and down the stairs to the hall.

His wellingtons were standing by the back door, and he pushed his feet into them, but he couldn't find his mackintosh anywhere. In the end, he took his mum's umbrella and his dad's big torch and opened the back door carefully.

The wind was roaring between the piles of junk, and it howled icily through the material of his pyjamas. He put up the umbrella and marched heroically across the yard, pushing his way against the wind and hearing the rain thunder down on the stretched cloth above his head.

When he got near the bath where they'd been sitting that afternoon, he heard another noise. There was the sound of the rain splashing into deep water, and the gurgle of water running down something, like a stream. He flashed the torch up towards the bath and saw water flooding in dozens of tiny tricklets off every surface and ledge of the nearby heaps. Most of it was splashing straight into the bath.

And in the bath, spinning and bobbing around like huge, dancing water lilies, were lots of floppy white things. All the pages they had written so carefully. Eight of Clipper's, five of Spag's and one of his own. Barny put the torch down on the ground and tried to pull the paper out of the water. But it was already soggy and, as he touched it, it fell into mushy pieces.

His teeth suddenly clicked together in a frozen chatter and he realised where he was. Standing outside in his pyjamas with only an umbrella

overhead. Must be mad! He bent down to pick up the torch and, as he did so, he saw another white thing underneath the bath, sheltered from the rain. It was Clipper's postcard with the ideas for saving the school. Even though it hardly seemed worth it at that moment, he picked it up before he straightened and scooted back to the house, muttering his way through the rain.

'Bet Shakespeare didn't have to sit in an old bath

to write his plays. An' if he did, I bet no one interrupted him with chocolate cake. An' if they did, I bet there was never floods while he was eating it. An' if there was ...'

4 · The Football Match

'But you've *got* to, Clipper!' Barny stopped walking along the road and turned to stare at her in horror. 'The Football Cup's the only thing left we can win. Our only chance to make the school famous and unshutdownable. If you don't play, it'll be a disaster.'

'It's worse than that,' Spag said gloomily, pulling leaves off the privet hedge next to him. 'If she doesn't play, *I'll* have to.'

'It's all right for you two to talk.' Clipper frowned and swung her bag round her head. 'You don't have to ask my mum. She gets so upset if I play football. She's funny like that.'

'I'll tell you what,' Barny said, struck by inspiration. 'We *will* ask your mum. We'll come and persuade her, Clipper. Tell her how much we need you in the team.'

He ran on towards Clipper's house and the three

48

of them filed in at the back door and stood in a row in the kitchen, staring hopefully at Clipper's mum. She was sitting listening to the radio and the music had just got to a loud bit, so she didn't bother to say hello. Just picked up three apples and threw one at each of them.

Barny bit his quickly, so that she wouldn't take it back. Then he yelled, 'We didn't come for that. We came to talk to you. Please!'

'Well now.' She reached across and clicked off

the radio, and then looked at them. 'If it's not food, what can it be? I wonder.'

'It's the Honour of the School,' Barny said importantly. 'We need Clipper after school tomorrow. We must have her.'

Clipper's mum sighed and looked at her daughter. 'Oh Caroline. It's the football again.'

Clipper stuck out her bottom lip and kicked at the kitchen mat. 'The Challenge Cup,' she muttered. 'First game of the series.'

Her mum sighed again and tugged gently at Clipper's hair. 'You're a hard one to bring up, you know,' she said. 'Five brothers is bad for making a girl grow up rough and tough. I've got to do something to soften you down, or you'll never grow up right.'

'Oh, *Mum!*' Clipper sniffed. 'I gave up fighting the boys when you said. Ask Gobbo. Ask Spag. But football – Oh, Mum.'

'Hmm.' Her mother looked thoughtful and began to eat an apple herself, without really noticing. 'I suppose it wouldn't really make any difference if –'

'*Please!*' Clipper said, her big brown eyes wide and pleading.

Her mum looked at her carefully, chewing as she made up her mind. Barny was growing impatient, and he thought it was time he said something himself.

'Oh, go on, Mrs Young. Let her play. Honestly, she's the toughest in the team. She's the best man we've got. No one else is such a hard tackler and – OW!'

The OW! was because Spag had kicked him hard on the ankle.

'Well now,' said Clipper's mother slowly, 'perhaps I don't want my only daughter to be a hard tackler.'

'Oh Mum,' said Clipper. But she sounded different this time. As if she knew it wouldn't do any good.

'You can watch, mind,' her mother said. 'In fact, I'll come and watch myself, seeing it's for the Honour of the School. But play you will not, Caroline. And, while I think of it, you can wear a dress to school tomorrow, instead of those trousers.'

'Oh, MUM!'

'If only you'd kept your mouth shut I wouldn't have had to play,' grumbled Spag as he pulled the number nine shirt over his head and tied on his glasses with string.

'Well, how was I to know?' Barny growled, tugging down the goalie's jersey, which hardly stretched round his stomach. 'Come on. We'll be late.'

The two of them jogged across to the park, where all the school matches were played. The first person they bumped into was Elaine Potter. With Sharon Grove, of course.

'I say – er – ' Spag leaned forward to whisper at them, 'I think you've made a *leetle* mistake. This

51

is a football match. You know, *football*. Mud and things. You don't like it.'

'Oh, you!' Sharon Grove went off into giggles, but Elaine sniffed and spat out her plaits.

'We're not here for the football. We don't watch football. But my mum's coming down. She said it would be a good chance to get some more parents for her procession.'

'Has she tried a fishing net?' Barny said helpfully. 'She could catch them in that and keep

them prisoners until the day. Then she could let them go one by one, so they made a procession, and – '

'Come on, Sharon,' said Elaine in a superior voice. 'Let's go and find someone sensible to talk to. And I don't mean that person in a dress over there.'

It was Clipper she meant, of course. She was right over the other side of the park, staring up into the big oak tree. Barny and Spag ran across to talk to her.

'What're you doing?' said Barny.

Clipper did not look round. 'Waiting for an acorn to fall in my eye,' she said sarcastically. 'What d'you think?'

Spag picked one up off the ground and flicked it at her. 'Happy now?'

'I'm waiting,' Clipper said slowly and crossly, 'for my mother. Because she said to meet her here. But if you think I'm going to stay and watch the rotten mess you'll all make of this Cup match, you've got another think coming.'

Barny felt an Idea coming on. He opened his mouth and it popped out. 'Hey, but you don't just have to stand and watch, do you? You can be the coach. Run up and down and tell everyone what to do. Like you always do. You just have to remember to keep off the pitch, that's all. Then you won't be playing.'

'Why not?' Clipper grinned suddenly and punched Barny. 'That's almost a good idea,

53

Gobbo. And I won't be playing if I give you some practice shots before the game starts either, will I? Come on!'

All sparked up, she raced off to pinch a ball from someone. Barny gave a little groan. She was a hard shooter.

'Get in goal, Gobbo,' Spag said, almost cheerfully. 'Let's see you stop a few of Clipper's blockbusters.'

Clipper was flashing up and down the pitch, dribbling the ball to get her feet in trim, but as soon as Barny got in between the posts she shot. The ball zoomed straight past his legs and he sat down with shock.

'Oh my,' Clipper said, 'you sure as eggs need some practice. Now!' And she began to shout.

She wasn't just the best tackler in the team. She was the best shouter, too. Better than Spotty McGrew, and much better than Mr Fox, who only shouted at people when their bootlaces were undone. By the time she had finished whizzing the ball from every side and yelling at Barny what to do, he actually managed to save a couple.

Clipper would have gone on, but just at that moment Elaine said in a loud voice. 'Oh, how nice! Clipper's mother's come to watch. What a pity Clipper isn't playing. At least, I *thought* she wasn't.'

Clipper did a quick snarl at her and went flying across to the far side of the pitch, so that she could scuff her shoes in the long grass and stop her mother seeing how muddy and footballish they were.

'Now,' said Barny to Spag, 'remember it's the Honour of the School. You've got to get goals, even if you don't like the thought.'

'It's not *thinking* I have problems with,' said Spag mournfully as he went lolloping up the pitch, ready for the starting whistle.

Barny took a deep breath and stuck his stomach out in a determined way, as though he could fill the whole goalmouth by puffing himself up. This was It. The Big Match. It was only the first one, but if they lost it they'd be out of the Cup. If they won it, they'd have beaten King's Road, the worst of their rivals, and they'd be well on the way to the semi-finals and –

'Spag!' yelled a voice in his right ear. 'Get in there with both feet, man. *Tackle!*'

It was Clipper, warming up. Obediently, Spag charged at one of the King's Road players, putting his head down like a mad bull. The King's Road boy just stuck out an arm. Spag bounced off it and sat down in the mud, looking rather surprised.

'Use your *feet*, boy!' bellowed Clipper. But before Spag could untangle his legs she was off up the sideline, following the ball and leaping up and down with impatience.

Barny could see Clipper's mum on the other side of the pitch, looking as if she wanted to get round and collar Clipper, to stop her shouting. But she couldn't, because she had been collared herself, by

Soppy Mrs Potter. All flapping hands and cooing, Mrs Potter was. Barny tried to overhear what they were saying, but just at that moment he heard Clipper yell, 'Gobbo!' and, automatically, he dived.

He nearly saved it. If his fingers had been half an inch longer, it would have been the save of the century. There was no need for Clipper to glare at him like that. There was certainly no need for Spotty McGrew to be shouting, 'You'd do better with two wet fish for hands!' Just wait till his fingers had grown to their proper length and he was keeping goal for England. He wouldn't sign any autographs for them. Then they'd be sorry.

At half-time, the Bennett School were still one–nil down. Clipper called them all round her in a huddle and gave one of her best encouraging speeches, but it didn't seem to cheer anyone up.

'Oh *Clip*!' Spotty McGrew said. 'Wouldn't your mum let you come on just as a sub in the second half?'

Clipper had a quick look across the pitch to check. But her mum was eyeing her as if she wanted to freeze her to the spot then and there. She shook her head. 'You'll just have to do it by yourselves. Come on, Spag. Pull yourself together.'

'Pull myself together *where*?' Spag said hopelessly.

But he tried harder in the second half. Barny could tell that he was trying harder. He kept racing up and down the pitch, panting like a hurricane.

56

The only trouble was that he kept losing track of the ball, so that he wasn't always running in the same direction as everyone else. And the string from his glasses gradually came untied and flapped behind him. In the end, it fell off altogether and wrapped itself round his feet. But he'd fallen over so many times by then that he didn't seem to care any more.

With only about five minutes to go, the Bennett forwards made a big push towards the King's Road goalmouth, with Clipper jumping up and down impatiently on the sideline. 'Come on, Spotty! Pass the ball! Get up there, Spag! You're supposed to be a forward! Unless you've got your jersey upside-down!'

Panting, but still trying hard, Spag began to pound up the pitch, just as the Bennett forwards lost the ball to the King's Road defenders. Barny saw all the other Bennett players droop a little, as if they were giving up. But not Spag. He didn't know where the ball was anyway. He was just trying to get up front.

As one of the enemy backs slipped the ball to their goalkeeper, Spag made a last desperate leap forward, tripped on his shoelace and fell headlong. Somehow, his forehead hit the moving ball with a terrific thwack. The ball bounced once, swerved round the goalie, and trickled into the back of the net.

'Spag!' chirped Clipper, bounding up and down like a maniac. 'You've done it! You've equalised!'

'Good old Spag!' yelled the rest of the Bennett team, crowding round him.

In the middle of the hustle, Spag peeled himself slowly off the mud and straightened up, blinking. 'Watch out for my glasses,' he said patiently. 'They fell off.'

Barny prowled up and down on the other goal line, feeling rather left out. Here he was, holding off the enemy attack and stopping all goals – well, almost all goals – but no one ever cheered him. And all Spag had to do was fall over. It really wasn't fair. They all ought to see how well he was playing. As the ball was kicked off for the last few minutes, he spread his shoulders and prepared to do a spectacular, leaping save.

But the ball didn't come towards him. It was booted off in the other direction, with Spag trailing well behind it, and Clipper bawling like a town-crier. Barny was left alone at his end of the pitch, imagining what a brilliant winning goal he would score if he weren't tied to the goal.

Bet I could beat all their defence, if I had to, he thought. All alone, swerving past one man, past another and another. And then – a fantastic shot from twenty yards, straight into the back of the net. He closed his eyes briefly, picturing it.

'Gobbo!' bellowed a desperate voice in his ear. He whirled round, but it was too late even to dive. The ball cannoned past him into his open goal. As his mouth fell open, the whistle shrieked, blowing for full-time.

5 · It Pays to Advertise – Or Does It?

'Well, Spag didn't do anything either,' Barny said sulkily at school next day. 'He just fell over his feet.'

'If *you'd* fallen over, we might have stood a bit more chance,' snarled Clipper. She was sitting with her back to a chimney-stack, staring at the ground in gloom.

'Oh, shut up,' said Spag cheerfully. 'That's all over. It's *my* idea now, and we can get properly organised.'

'Get more children?' Barny snorted. 'That's not really an idea. It's just a joke.'

But Spag was too busy to be annoyed. He put his hand into his pocket and pulled out a bundle of papers. 'I've written everything out in detail. With copies. Look, this is what we're going to do.'

Clipper began to read the piece of paper he gave her. After a moment, she gulped and looked up again. 'You're mad,' she said. 'You've *got* to be mad!'

Her face was horrified.

It looked even more horrified on Saturday morning when Barny and Spag got to the cinema. They could see her lurking down the alley at the side of the building. She was peering anxiously round the corner, but the rest of her body was hidden, huddled up against the wall. Spag marched determinedly up to her.

'Right, Clipper. Ready to start?'

'Honest?' she said in a thin voice. 'You really mean it? In front of all those people?'

Spag sighed and started to talk in his annoying lecturing voice. 'Look, it's perfectly logical. We want more children to come to our school, don't we? Well, I explained it all before. It's just like everything else. What do you do if you want people to come to a circus or something? You advertise!'

Clipper opened the front of her raincoat a crack and looked down doubtfully at what she was wearing. 'Yes, I know, but I still don't see what all that's got to do with me wearing this rubbish. I look a proper idiot.'

Spag sighed again, more noisily. 'Clipper! I've told you. They're not going to hear what we've got to say unless they're listening. That's what you're going to do. You're going to attract their attention. Then I say what it's all about. And then we give them something to remember it by.'

'I'm quite enough to remember all by myself,' said Clipper gloomily, taking off her raincoat. Underneath, she was wearing a frilly ballet dress that Spag's sister had worn when she was a fairy in a school play. On her legs she wore a pair of glittery silver tights that Barny had borrowed from his mother without asking. The tights were too big and they sagged into sloppy wrinkles round her knees. Miserably, she hitched them up and peered round the corner at the long queue of children lined up by the door of the cinema, waiting for the Saturday morning pictures to start. 'I couldn't do it in my raincoat, could I?'

'Clipper!' Spag said, exasperated, 'You can't change it now. We've planned it. *Go on!*' He gave her a hard shove and she staggered out of the end of the alley on to the pavement in full view of all the queueing children and the passing shoppers.

'Hello, children!' she squeaked, in a bright, wobbly voice. All the passing people stopped in amazement, leaving a clear space along the edge of the pavement. Along this strip, Clipper started to do handsprings, her glittery legs and frilly skirts whirling dazzlingly round and round.

Spag's plan said that she should do six handsprings and then straighten up with a flourish and announce that he was going to speak to the children. Unfortunately for the plan, Clipper was very happy doing handsprings. As long as she was twirling over and over, she didn't have to stand still in the fancy dress and watch people staring at

61

her. So she went on handspringing along the pavement, right past the cinema queue.

But she was stopped in the end. In mid-spring, when she was upside-down, she cannoned into a fat, red-faced woman with three parcels and a shopping trolley. Over in a heap went Clipper and over went the fat woman, looking surprised and furious. Oranges, buns, tins of beans and packets of washing powder cascaded everywhere and rolled along the pavement.

Spag decided that he had better get on with the next bit of his advertisement, before the fat woman recovered and started to shout. He jumped out of the end of the alley and shouted brightly, just as Clipper had, 'Hello, children!'

All the heads in the queue swivelled towards him, grinning and eager to see who was going to be knocked over next. Seizing his chance, Spag began in his loudest voice, 'This is important to you!'

For a moment or two, Barny huddled in the alley. Then he poked his head round the corner to see how it was going.

It wasn't going very well. The children had been quite happy to watch Clipper knock people over, but they didn't see why they should stand quietly and let Spag tell them what a good school he went to. They all began to yell at him.

'Yah! Ours is better'n that!'

'Get back to your dustbin!'

'Everyone knows the Bennett's a rotten hole!'

63

Spag's long, bony face went hot pink. 'We need more children!' he spluttered bravely.

'Huh!' The fat woman looked up from where she was grovelling on the pavement, gathering up her shopping. 'Hope there's no more like *her*! More *police*, that's what we want.'

'Children!' Spag went on heroically, 'you should tell your mums and dads – '

Barny decided that the time had come for him to take a hand. No one at all was listening to Spag. And any minute now the fat woman would call a policeman, or the cinema doors would open and the queue would disappear inside. Before they got to the Something To Remember bit. The bit Barny was in. He charged out of the alley, yelling, 'Come on, Clipper, let's do the song now.'

Clipper ran across to Spag, with her teeth clenched. She looked a bit odd, because her fancy dress was covered in tomato ketchup and HP Sauce from the fat woman's broken bottles, but she came when he called. That was the good thing about Clipper. She never gave up when things got tough.

'Let's give it to them,' she said determinedly.

They straightened into a line, facing the cinema queue, and, as loudly as they could manage, they began to sing the jingle that Spag had made up for his advertisement.

> *If you want to pass the test,*
> *The Bennett Junior is the best!*

> *If you don't go to the Bennett School,*
> *You may grow up to be a fool!'*

'Here!' shouted one spotty boy at the front of the queue. 'Who d'you think you're calling a fool?'

'Yeah,' said another boy, 'think we're stupid or summink?'

The whole cinema queue yelled, in a racket of enraged voices, and hurtled suddenly forwards as all the children launched themselves towards Barny, Clipper and Spag. Bodies crashed together, with those children who didn't go to the Bennett fighting those who did, and those who didn't even know what the fight was about punching away just for the love of it.

Slowly, the whole struggling group of children heeled over and fell in a heap of thrashing arms and legs that covered the entire stretch of pavement.

And underneath the heap, at the very bottom, was Barny, muttering, 'Bet no one ever got in a mess like this advertising baked beans. An' if they did – '

He didn't get any further, because something hard and spiky suddenly dug into his leg, through all the layers of the scrum. Someone was standing over the children, prodding with an umbrella and saying in a shrill voice, 'Children you must stop this! Stop it at once!'

Whoever she was, no one took any notice of her. They were all enjoying themselves too much. The wrestling went on until a different, deeper voice

65

boomed over the writhing bodies. Even from under three layers of people, Barny recognised it. It was the voice of the cinema manager, who yelled at the children every Saturday morning to keep them in order.

'No one want the cinema, then?' he shouted. 'I'm going to shut the doors in *five minutes*!'

There was a gigantic scrabble, with legs flying in all directions, as the children picked themselves off the heap and raced into the cinema foyer. In thirty seconds, there were only three people left sitting on the pavement. Barny, Spag and Clipper.

Clipper had a dreamy, blissful look on her face. 'Best fight I've been in for years,' she said. 'Why did someone have to come and break it up?'

'Hey!' The spiky umbrella prodded Barny in the back. 'Aren't you three going to thank me for saving you?'

Oh no. It was Soppy Mrs Potter. And there beside her was her rotten daughter with a smug, goody-goody expression on her face.

'Well,' said Mrs Potter grimly, 'what on earth have you been up to?'

'It was just Spag's stupid idea for saving the school,' said Clipper wearily. 'And it didn't work, did it?'

To Barny's horror, Mrs Potter's disapproving expression suddenly changed into a delighted, beaming smile. 'You dear children!' she cooed. 'How marvellous to find you care!' She lowered her umbrella to rest on the ground and began to rummage in her bag. 'You must all come on my procession. I'll write down the details for you.'

While she wasn't looking, Clipper stuck out her tongue at Elaine, as far as it would go. Elaine replied by waggling her hands at her ears and going cross-eyed. But by the time her mother looked up, she had returned to her usual sickly, angelic expression.

'There you are, dears.' Mrs Potter thrust her bit of paper at Barny. 'I'll see you all next Saturday. To carry on the good fight. Mind you're there.'

Luckily, she and Elaine went off at that point, otherwise she would have heard Clipper's groans.

Spag wasn't taking any notice of anybody. He sat in the middle of the pavement, with his chin resting on his knees, staring gloomily at the toes of his dusty plimsolls.

'Should have known it wouldn't work,' he muttered. 'Should have guessed it would be a disaster.'

But Barny had started to smile. He suddenly felt another idea coming on. A super, splendiferous idea. His eyes gleamed and he stared off into the distance, past Spag and Clipper, and past Woolworths, up the hill.

'Procession,' he said dreamily. 'Float.'

'Float?' said Spag.

'*Float?*' Clipper looked at him. 'What d'you think we are? Rubber ducks?'

'Not that kind of float, you idiot. The other kind. You know.' He flapped his hands impatiently. 'Like they have at carnivals. With Beauty Queens and people dressed up and bands and things.'

'Poor old Gobbo.' Spag shook his head sadly. 'It's happened at last. He's gone completely nutty.'

'Screwy,' said Clipper.

'Insane.'

'Off his rocker.'

'SHUT UP!' Barny clapped a fat hand over each of their mouths. 'Just because you've got no brains, there's no need to go on at me.'

'But you need a lorry for a float,' Spag said gently. 'A great big ten ton truck.'

'Not in my idea.' Barny gave a smug grin. 'Come round next Saturday morning. About half past nine. Then you'll see. You bring your bike,

Spag. Oh, and Clipper had better bring her swimming costume.'

'I thought floats didn't need any water,' Clipper said sarcastically. 'What's it all about, Gobbo?'

But Barny wouldn't tell them. He just hummed mysteriously as they went back to Clipper's house.

6 · Clipper Rides in Style

'Gobbo!' said Clipper, standing in the entrance of the yard. '*Gob*bo, Gob*bo*, Go-o-o-o-obbo! We're here! *We're* here! We're *here*! We're h – '

'Shut up!' hissed Barny, poking his head out from behind a pile of rusty old lawn-mowers. 'My mum hasn't gone out yet.'

'What's that got to do with it?' Spag parked his bike carefully round the side of the house, where it couldn't possibly get mixed up with any of the heaps in the yard. Then he tiptoed round to join Barny behind the lawn-mowers. Swinging her scarlet swimming costume from one finger, Clipper joined them.

'Well?' she said.

'We've got to wait till my mum goes out,' Barny whispered, 'because we're going to make our float out of the junk. And you know what will happen if she finds out.'

'Tornado,' said Clipper sympathetically.

Spag nodded. 'Hurricane and earthquake.'

'That's right,' Barny said. 'So she *mustn't* find out.'

'And I suppose your dad doesn't mind?' Spag said in gloomy disbelief. 'Suppose he'll come out here and tell us we can play with all the junk we want. Why should he care? It's only his living. He'll adore having us steal it all.'

'Sssh!' muttered Barny urgently. 'It's all right. He's asleep. He won't wake up till lunch-time. And we're not stealing the junk. Just borrowing it.'

'Well, how – '

'Sssh! Here comes my mum.'

The huge, square figure of Mrs Gobbo, wrapped in her fur coat, came hurrying out of the kitchen door. The great expanse of brown fur made her look a bit like a grizzly bear on the prowl. She stood in the middle of the yard and let out a hoarse whisper that carried for yards.

'Barny! Don't forget your breakfast. There's porridge in the oven, and you can do bacon and eggs and sausages. And mushrooms if you want. And there's lots of toast and marmalade. But don't wake your dad.'

'No, Mum. Bye,' Barny shouted, without coming out of his hiding place.

'Goluptious!' Clipper licked her lips and looked after Mrs Gobbo's departing figure. 'I love your mum when she's in a good mood. Don't you think

71

we ought to have breakfast before we start? I only had cornflakes and a boiled egg and – '

'No,' said Barny firmly. 'We've only got an hour and a bit before the procession starts. We've got to get going. Over here.'

He waved towards a corner of the yard, where there was a heap of old pram wheels. 'Those. And a bath.'

'A bath?' Clipper looked at him. Then she looked down at her swimming costume. 'That Gobbo,' she said loudly to no one in particular, 'he *surely* thinks floats have got something to do with water.'

'No I don't!' Barny ruffled up his hair and looked at her in exasperation. 'Can't you see? I'm serious. We tie the bath on top of two sets of pram wheels and there's our float. You can see, can't you, Spag?'

Spag was frowning across at the feet of the old bath they'd used as a den. 'What d'you think we are? Heavyweight champions of the world? We'll never shift that old bath around. It's made of cast iron. Must weigh a ton.'

'Not *that* bath,' Barny said, almost gibbering with impatience. 'You know this yard is full of baths. Look, we're going to use that one. Over there.'

He pointed to another corner. There, standing on one end, was a much smaller, more modern bath. It was a virulent, startling shade of purple.

'Oh my,' Clipper said, wrinkling up her face, 'they'll certainly see us coming.'

'Hmm.' Spag walked up to the bath and surveyed it. 'Yes, I reckon we could get that tied up. But what do we do when we've got it on the wheels? Push it?'

Barny suddenly looked very pleased with himself. 'No, we don't push it. We tow it. You and me. We tie it behind our bikes.'

'Hey!' All at once, Spag got the idea. He was as near being excited as he ever got. Fetching two sets of wheels, he put them side by side and looked at the bath. 'What're we going to fix it with?'

'Got a couple of bits of rope.' Barny carried them over. He was all ready to organise the other two and give orders to them. After all, it was his idea. But somehow it was Clipper and Spag who took charge. Spag got busy working out the best way to space the wheels and Clipper tied the knots with her tough little fingers, wherever he told her. Clipper was the best at knots in the whole school. Everyone knew that. Ever since the day in the Infants when she'd tied up Elaine with five skipping ropes and it had taken Mr Pratt an hour to undo her.

At first Barny flapped round, trying to help them, but he only got in the way. Spag bumped into him and Clipper fell over him and they both shouted. In the end, he stood back and let them get on with it. After all, he was the one who had the ideas. It was only right for them to do the work.

73

'There!' Clipper sat back on her heels and looked at the float with pride. 'Bet those knots won't come undone in a hurry.'

The purple bath was lashed securely to the wheels, with a loop of rope over each end. In front, two lengths of rope were attached, one to Spag's rusty old bike and the other to Barny's shiny new one.

Clipper went on beaming at her work for a moment. Then, suddenly, she frowned. 'There's only one thing I don't understand.' She fished up the scarlet swimming costume, which had got trampled underfoot while they were working. 'What's this for?'

'Well – er – um – ' Barny looked away from her and rubbed his nose.

'Barny Gobbo!' Clipper got up suspiciously. 'What's going on in that so-called brain of yours?'

'Well – ' Barny slipped round to the other side of the bath, so that it was safely between them. 'I thought you could put it on and – and – go in the back and be a Beauty Queen.'

'*Gobbo!*' Clipper launched herself at him, straight across the top of the float, but Spag caught at her arms and pulled her back.

'Come on, Clipper. You'll only break the float. And someone's got to go in the back of the float. You can't have a float with nobody in it.'

'But why's it always got to be me? I did that rotten thing with the fairy dress. Why has it got to be me that does this as well?'

'You're the only one without a bike,' Spag said reasonably.

'Huh! I could just as well ride one of yours.' Clipper kicked sulkily at the pram wheels. 'Well, I won't do it. So there.'

'But Clipper, you must!' Barny was ready to launch into an argument, but Spag winked at him over Clipper's head.

'Course,' he said thoughtfully, 'we could always ask Soppy Elaine, couldn't we, Gobbo? She'd love us to pull her round the town in her swimming costume.'

'Yes.' Barny grinned back at him. 'And she's got long hair, if she undoes her plaits.'

'*She's* not doing it!' Clipper said fiercely. 'I haven't got long hair, but at least mine's not chewed.'

'You'll do it then?' Barny said quickly.

Clipper sighed and shook some of the dust off her hair. 'I'll go in and change.'

Five minutes later she came out again, her lean, wiry body dressed in a bright red costume. 'There,' she said crossly. 'I hope you're happy now. I think it's a daft idea. No one would think I was meant to be a Beauty Queen. I look more like a channel swimmer.'

Barny looked at her, considering. 'I know,' he said, 'Wait a minute.'

He ran into the house and came back with a little bag, a long white scarf, and pair of his mum's high-heeled shoes. 'Here.' He thrust the shoes at

75

Clipper, who pulled a face as she slipped her feet into them. They were about five sizes too big. Barny ignored her expression. 'Got to have a sash, too. They always have sashes.' He draped the scarf under her opposite arm. 'Good thing I brought Mum's lipstick.' He pulled it out of the little make-up bag and used it to write MISS BENNETT SCHOOL along the sash.

'Your mum's going to be pleased,' Spag said.

Barny flapped a hand. 'Oh, I'll wash it or something before she gets back. Now I'm going to put some lipstick on Clipper.'

Clipper pulled a face, but she stood obediently while Barny smeared the lipstick over her mouth. It was bright scarlet like her swimsuit.

'Whoops!' he said. 'The end of this is a bit rough from writing on the sash. There you are, Clipper. It's gone over the edges a bit.'

'Let's have a look.' Clipper ferreted in the make-up bag. 'There must be a mirror in here somewhere.' She fished it out, looked in it, and pulled a disgusted face. 'I look as if I've had an accident with a jam sandwich.'

'Oh, do stop fussing, Clipper,' Barny said. 'It'll have to do, or we'll never be at the procession in time. Now, help us get this float out of the gate.'

It was a bit awkward, because the ropes attached to the bikes kept getting tangled round bits of junk. Everyone had to dart about and catch things before they clanged to the ground and woke Barny's dad. But at last the float was outside in the road, with

the two bikes ahead of it, facing up the hill that lay between them and the town centre. Clipper jumped into the purple bath and struck a dramatic pose.

'Right, slaves,' she shouted. 'Take me to the procession.'

Barny and Spag climbed on to their bikes and pushed at the pedals as hard as they could.

Nothing happened.

'Come on, swabs,' said Clipper. 'Put some beef into it.'

Still nothing happened.

'It's no good, Clip,' Spag said at last. 'It's the hill. You'll have to get out and push.'

'Push? But I'm supposed to be a Beauty Queen. That's what you said. Beauty Queens don't push baths.'

'Only to the top of the hill.' Spag eyed the slope. 'We'll be all right going down the other side into the town.'

Grumbling under her breath, Clipper got out and put her shoulder to the back of the bath.

'One, two, three, *heave*!' she called.

She strained against the purple edge of the bath with all her might. At the front, Barny and Spag stood up, putting their full weight on their pedals. Slowly, the float began to move up the hill. The slope had never seemed so long or so steep, but at last the bath was on top, on the flat bit. Peering down the other side, into the town, the three of them could see the people beginning to gather for

78

the procession outside the Town Hall, at the bottom of the hill. Nobody was looking up the hill towards them.

'Right, let's go and give them a surprise,' Barny said. 'It looks like a pretty boring old procession. I should think they'd be glad to have us to liven it up. Get in, Clipper.'

Clipper jumped in and took up her grand pose again. 'It would be better with horses to pull it.'

'It would be better with a proper Beauty Queen,' muttered Spag.

'Shut up, you two,' Barny said. 'Let's start. One, two, *three*!'

Spag and Barny pushed down on their pedals, and this time it worked. Slowly the float started to move along the flat road towards the downward slope. Barny grinned with satisfaction to see his idea working.

'Good, isn't it?'

'The only way to travel,' grunted Clipper.

Barny looked over his shoulder. 'Clipper! What are you doing?' She was standing squarely in the bath, flexing her muscles. 'You're supposed to be a Beauty Queen. You look like Tarzan. Stop it!'

'Oh, all right,' Clipper said sulkily. She stood sideways and put on a silly simper. 'That better?'

Spag glanced back. 'Have to do,' he said casually. 'It's a pity you're so ugly.'

He pedalled even harder down the hill, chuckling to hear Clipper screaming with rage because she couldn't get at him.

But, after a second or two, he stopped chuckling and looked nervously back again. 'Er – Barny?'

'Yes?' Barny had half shut his eyes and was free-wheeling delightedly down the hill.

Spag coughed anxiously. 'We haven't got any brakes on this thing, you know.'

'Brakes?' Barny opened both eyes wide in surprise. 'What do we want brakes for? We had enough trouble getting it going at all.'

'That was going *up*hill,' Spag said in a voice of doom. 'We're going *down*hill now.'

Suddenly Clipper squealed from behind. 'Can't you two go any faster? I'm catching you up!'

'No, we can't,' Spag said sharply. 'We're free-wheeling.' His face was all screwed up, as if he were inventing a way for them to stop, but before he could finish his plan things started to happen quickly.

Clipper screamed, 'I'm coming pa-a-ast!'

Spag swerved out sideways, so that she wouldn't bump into the back of them, and the heavy bath, which had been gathering speed all the way down the hill, zoomed through the gap.

The people who had collected for the procession certainly looked round when they heard Clipper's yell. They saw a bright purple bath hurtling towards them between two bicycles. Standing in the bath, holding on frantically with both hands, was a small figure in a bright scarlet swimsuit, with a glaring red mouth.

The crowd began to scatter uneasily, but it was

too late. The bath ploughed sideways into a lamp-post. Clipper shot out like a cannonball, straight towards a fat woman whose arms were loaded with parcels. For a moment, Barny could see the woman's eyes widen in disbelief. It was the fat woman from outside the cinema. Then Clipper, the woman and the parcels collapsed into a jumbled heap against the rest of the crowd, knocking over the people behind them. Into the muddle of arms and legs ploughed Spag and Barny, still frantically squeezing their bicycle brakes.

The fat woman raised her head wearily and peered at Clipper. 'Can't you find something else to do on Saturday mornings?' she said.

Barny lifted his head half an inch from the tangle of bodies and cycle wheels he was in and opened one eye cautiously. He could see Mrs Potter looking speechless with rage at having her procession spoilt. And next to her was Elaine, doubled up with silent, gloating laughter. Barny put his head down again and shut his eyes. Perhaps he'd pretend to be unconscious.

But it was too late. Someone had seen him. The crowd swayed and parted as a massive square figure in a fur coat pushed through. With a last gigantic step over the fat lady, Barny's mum caught hold of him by the scruff of his neck, pulling him out of the jumble of machinery and people.

'Well?' she said.

7 · Barny's Secret Idea

Clipper knelt on the floor in Spag's sitting room and began to turn out her pockets all over the tidy carpet. She pulled out toffees, a luminous transfer – which she promptly stuck on her forehead – a penknife with a broken blade and four Football Superstars cards. She was looking for the battered, old half-postcard with their Plan written on it.

'Here it is,' she said at last. 'There's not much left we haven't done, though. Only Gobbo's Secret Idea. And that's bound to mean more trouble.'

'No, come on.' Spag stretched out his legs and leaned back expectantly. 'Tell us what this brilliant idea is, Gobbo.'

'Well – er – ' Barny went pink and shuffled his bottom about in his chair.

'I don't think he's got an idea at all,' Clipper said scornfully.

'Yes I have!'

'Well, get on with it then,' Spag drawled.

'Or I'll sit on your head,' threatened Clipper.

'Well – what I thought of was a sit-in,' Barny said slowly. When they didn't hurrah straight away, he went on talking as fast as he could, to convince them. 'You know. We stay in the school and refuse to come out until they promise not to knock it down. Like on the television. You must have seen them.'

'But – ' Spag frowned and hugged the back of his neck. 'If we sit in the school, they'll just pick us up and dump us outside.'

'I've thought of that,' Barny said, pleased with himself. 'We can chain ourselves to something with our bicycle padlocks.'

'But,' Spag had on his practical, discouraging face now, 'we won't have time to padlock ourselves to anything. You know how quickly old Pratt turfs us out if he catches us loitering after school. We won't have a chance.'

For a moment Barny faltered. Then he said stoutly, 'We'll just have to get into the school when no one's about then.'

'Oh yes,' said Spag sarcastically. '*Ho* yes. Can't I just see us. Stocking masks over our faces, doing a break-in. You know what your trouble is, don't you Gobbo? No brains.' And he went rolling round in his chair muttering '*Ho* ho. *Ho* ho,' in a voice like disaster.

But Clipper was sitting up rigidly straight, her hands gripping her knees and her dark eyes glittering in an overheated way. 'You know,' she said carefully, 'there's something I've been wanting to do for *centuries*. Since last Friday at least. Look.'

She turned over the grey, battered piece of postcard and began to draw on the back. 'You know that shelter thing down by the Infants' entrance? Leaning up against the school wall?'

She sketched it. It looked more like a comb, but they knew what she meant. The shelter had a sloping metal roof, jutting out from the back wall of the school, supported by slim metal pillars. The Infants huddled miserably underneath it when it rained before school.

'Well,' said Clipper, 'I've been looking at it. I reckon I could shin up those pillars. And then climb up the sloping roof.'

'But that's no good,' Spag snatched the pencil. 'Look, when you've got to the top of the sloping roof, in front of you – here – there's only a blank wall.'

'Yes *but*.' Clipper snatched the pencil back. 'You haven't looked like I have. On the wall, just there, there's a sort of ornamental ledge. If I can shuffle along that, to the corner, just round the corner,' here she drew a few incomprehensible lines, 'there's a big window.'

'And?' said Spag.

'And,' said Clipper triumphantly, 'the catch is broken. I noticed it last Friday. It would be simple to open it from outside. Then I could let you two in at one of the downstairs windows.'

85

'Hmm.' Spag stared thoughtfully at the untidy drawing.

'Well?' Clipper turned to Barny. 'What do you think, master-brain?'

Barny was feeling excited about the way things were working themselves out. 'You can really do it?'

'Course I can,' Clipper said airily. 'My mum says I'm a monkey really, only nobody's noticed.'

'I thought *everyone* had noticed,' murmured Spag. Clipper flew at him and sat on his chest while he punched her from all sides with his long arms.

'Oh dear!' said Spag's mother weakly, looking round the door. 'What *are* you doing? And what's that heap of rubbish on the carpet, Caroline?'

By the time she had flapped them all out and they'd marched back to Barny's yard, somehow it was all settled. On Friday night the three of them would break into the school.

Friday night was very dark. As Barny crept out of bed, sneaked past the sitting room where his parents were watching television and slipped out into the yard, he thought it must be the darkest night for years. For centuries. A record.

He met the other two round the back of the school, and the three of them stood there, peering up at the shadowy building, while Spag flashed his torch along the route Clipper meant to climb. The school loomed huge and black, looking about five times as tall as it did in the daylight. The little ledge at the top of the sloping roof seemed very tiny.

'Clipper,' Spag said quietly, 'you don't have to.'

'Shut up,' said Clipper. Her voice was a bit tense, but she spat on her hands with a fine flourish. 'Here we go then.'

'Don't fall,' muttered Barny.

'I never fall. Have you ever seen me fall?' Clipper said confidently. She walked up to the metal pillar nearest the corner, glanced quickly up and down it, and then gave a light-footed jump. Catching the pillar with her hands, knees and feet, she started to push with her legs and pull with her arms, heaving herself upwards.

'The metal's *freezing*,' they heard her whisper. A moment later, she was hauling herself over the edge of the roof to lie along one of its supporting ribs.

'Well, that's the easy bit over anyway,' muttered Spag grimly. Looking sideways at him, Barny saw that he was biting his nails. What was he so worried about? For years the two of them had been watching Clipper climb up things – trees, lamp-posts, heaps of junk. And she was right. She never did fall. There didn't seem to be anything different about this.

But when Clipper reached the top of the sloping roof and stepped on to the little ledge, Barny suddenly realised what was making Spag twitch. From down below, it seemed that she was standing on nothing. Her small brown figure was spread-

87

eagled against the huge, blank wall, almost invisible
in the shadows, unless you knew where to look.
Barny gave an automatic gasp.

'Shut up!' hissed Spag, plastering a bony hand
across his mouth. 'Don't make a sound. If she falls
now, she'll kill herself.'

From way above their heads, a thin whisper
floated down. 'Can't see. Shine the torch, Spag.'

Spag switched it on and pointed the beam at the
ledge in front of Clipper's feet. For a moment the

light shook wildly as he trembled, and then he steadied the torch with his other hand and moved it slowly as Clipper moved.

The two boys stood side by side, without a word, watching Clipper edge and edge and edge up to the corner and carefully round it, until she came to the window. It was a big sash window and she caught hold of the bottom rim of the top part to steady herself. To open it, she had to bend down and pull up the bottom sash. Very, very slowly she bent over.

'If it comes open with a jerk,' Spag muttered, so softly that Barny could hardly hear, 'it'll push her off the ledge.' His voice was choky, as if he could hardly breathe properly.

All they could see was Clipper's bent figure, one hand clutching at the upper sash and the other fumbling at the bottom of the window. Barny shut his eyes for a second. The strain of peering into the darkness was making the shadows dance about. When he looked again, the window was open and Clipper was just stepping through into the black beyond. There was a quick flutter as she waved at them, and then she disappeared.

With a sound like balloons going down, Spag and Barny let out their breaths. They had been keeping utterly still while Clipper opened the window. But she had done it. She was in safely. The relief was so great that they started to laugh softly and punch each other.

'How about that, then?'

'Climbing Clipper, the Death-defying Dare-devil!'

They capered round in the shadow of the building until a furious voice hissed at them, 'If you don't shut up, you'll have Mr Pratt here with seventeen policemen. Get inside.'

It was Clipper, waving at them from the window of one of the Infants' classrooms. 'Come on.'

She hauled them through the window, then shut it and turned round with a swagger. 'Well, wasn't I fantastic?'

'Just like a monkey,' Spag said solemnly.

Barny straightened up and peered through the darkness at her. 'Weren't you scared, Clipper?'

'Scared? Me?' She chuckled. 'I'm never scared.'

'Not even a little bit?'

'Well.' She gave another chuckle. 'When I got inside I had to sit down for a minute before I could walk down the stairs. My knees went all wobbly.'

Barny knew what she meant. His own knees still felt rather funny, and he hadn't even done the climbing. For a moment – just a moment – while she was up there, he'd wondered if they were all mad. All this just for rotten old school. When they could all have been safe home in bed, in the warm.

He shook off the feeling. He was getting as soft as Elaine. Clipper and Spag were waiting for him to take charge and get his idea properly started.

'Right, men – ouch, *Clipper*!' He rubbed his head. 'Let's get going.'

90

'Going where?' Spag said in an odd voice, as though something had just occurred to him.

'I told you,' Barny said patiently. 'We're going to go upstairs. To our classroom, because it's got all those old pipes in the corner. And we're going to chain ourselves to the pipes, so no one can pull us away.'

'Yes,' said Spag, 'but what then?'

'Well, nothing. I've explained, Spag. If only you'd listen. We haven't got to do anything after that. We just sit tight and let everyone else do the fussing. All we've got to do is say we won't move until they agree not to close the school.'

'Yes, but,' Spag said, in gloomy triumph, 'who is this everyone? We've been so busy working out how to get into the school without being stopped that we haven't thought about how to tell people. Nobody knows we're here at all.'

There was a short prickly silence. Then Barny said awkwardly, 'We could telephone someone from the Head Mister's office.'

'It'll be locked,' grunted Spag.

Clipper flipped upside-down and walked round the classroom on her hands. 'Don't be so boring,' said her voice from the floor. 'We can write letters or something in the classroom and sneak out to post them.'

'Yes.' Barny was enthusiastic again. 'We can write to the Queen and the Prime Minister and the television and – '

'Oh, come on!' Clipper sprang the right way up

again and made for the door. 'Don't just stand there. I want to get to the chaining ourselves up bit.'

She pattered out and up the stairs and by the time Spag and Barny panted into the classroom she had already turned on the light, got paper and pencil out of her desk and was unwrapping a skipping rope from round her waist.

'Oh goody goody,' muttered Spag. 'You going to do *Salt, Mustard, Vinegar, Pepper*?'

'Don't be stupid,' Clipper sat down by the pipes which ran along one wall. 'Haven't got a bicycle, have I? So I haven't got a bicycle lock to chain myself up.' She started to wind the rope round and round her leg and the pipe, tying it as she went. 'They won't get me out of here in a hurry. Not with my knots.'

Spag pulled a shiny length of chain out of his pocket and stared at it. 'Four, five, two, six,' he muttered. 'Four, five, two, six. Four, five, two, six.'

Barny stared at him. 'What're you doing?'

'Combination of my padlock,' Spag said briefly. 'Look an idiot, won't I, if I forget it? Be stuck in here for life. Four, five, two, six.'

'*I've* got a key.'

'Bet you lose it. Four, five, two, six.'

'Shut up, you two,' said Clipper. 'I'm trying to write a letter to the Queen. If you go on yacking I'll make a spelling mistake or something.'

'I'll do the Prime Minister.' Barny sat down

quickly and wrapped his cycle lock round his leg and round the pipe. He clicked it shut.

'Oh, brilliant,' said Spag glumly. 'That leaves me the television, I suppose. How do I start that one? Dear Television?'

'Shut *up*!' Clipper was writing on her lap, her legs stuck straight out in front of her. 'Get that lock on and get writing.'

Five minutes later she put down her pencil. 'Done it! It's a great letter! Shall I read it to you?'

'No,' said Spag.

Clipper stretched out a foot and kicked him. 'Here goes then.' She cleared her throat importantly. 'Dear Your Majesty – '

Spag spluttered. 'You can't start like that!'

Clipper looked injured. 'Why not? What would you put?'

'Your Dear Majesty,' said Spag.

'Dear Queen,' Barny said.

'Your Majesty.'

'O Queen.'

Flapping her piece of paper, Clipper started reading again in an even louder voice. 'Dear Your Majesty – '

'Expecting someone royal?' said a heavy voice from the door.

'Oh!' All three of them gasped, and Clipper gave a little wriggle. Standing massively in the classroom doorway was Mr Pratt, the caretaker, his bald-headed face tangled into a fierce frown. He

93

lumbered across the classroom in four steps and stood looming over them.

'Come on. Out. Don't know how you got in here, but you know you got no business here. Not at this time of night. On your feet.'

The three of them sat up straighter and stared obstinately at him.

'What's keeping you, then? Little hooligans. I know who you are. Got all your names and addresses. Just wait till I tell Mr Jarvis on Monday.'

'Go on, Gobbo,' hissed Clipper. 'Tell him.'

'Tell him.' Spag kicked out at Barny. 'It's your idea.'

Barny gulped, went pink, and stammered, 'You – you won't need to tell him on Monday. We'll still be here. We're sitting in. To save the school. We're not going until they promise not to close it.'

Mr Pratt stared at them. His face went purple and his mouth dropped open.

'Don't you want to save the school?' Clipper said sweetly.

'Hrmmph!' Mr Pratt coughed in an embarrassed way. 'What I think's got nothing to do with it. Can't have you children in here. If you don't get out now, I'll have to pick you up and throw you out.'

Spag looked at him and shook his head. 'Take another look.' He wobbled his leg, jangling the links of his chain. 'We're fixed.'

'Attached.' Clipper twirled the end of her skipping rope at him.

'We – ' Barny tried to sound as brave as they did. 'We're not going away.'

'Hrmmph!' said Mr Pratt again. 'You'd better – ' He looked as if he were going to start yelling at them, but suddenly he changed his mind. He turned round and stomped out of the room.

'Well,' said Spag, 'that's solved one of our problems. At least someone knows we're here.'

'Yes, but what's he up to?' Barny said. 'That's what's worrying me.'

Clipper tightened her knots thoughtfully. 'He's gone off for reinforcements. What d'you think he'll bring? A posse of policemen?'

'More likely to be a ton of teachers,' muttered Spag. 'Or a heaviness of headmasters.'

Barny sat with his head back and stared at the ceiling, wishing he could joke like them. He knew who he'd fetch if he were Mr Pratt. And it wouldn't be teachers or policemen or headmasters. Suddenly, all the fun seemed to go out of the sit-in. Clipper dropped her letter to the floor and they sat silently waiting, not looking at each other.

They did not have to wait long. Footsteps began to sound. They came up and up and up, and then along the corridor. Mr Pratt appeared in the doorway again.

'Now you'll catch it,' he said cheerfully. We'll sort you all out double quick now. Come on, ladies.'

96

Barny looked through the doorway. He could see at once that he'd been right. Mr Pratt had done just what he'd been afraid of. He bent his head and groaned.

It was all their mothers. Spag's mother looked flappy and fussy. Clipper's mother looked thoughtful and worried. Barny's mother just looked huge. Barny clenched his fists and waited for the bellowing to start.

But everything was very quiet. The mothers stared at them for a moment. Then Mrs Barlow ruffled her hair distractedly and shook her head at Spag. 'I can't understand it. Oh dear, I just can't understand it at all. I've never had any trouble with James before, and now all of a sudden he – '

'It's the school, Mum,' Spag said patiently. 'I told you about it. We don't want it knocked down by bulldozers.'

'I wish I knew,' his mother said. Her voice faded away.

'What *I'd* like to know,' put in Mr Pratt weightily, 'is how the little perishers got in. I locked the place up when I went off, same as usual. More locked up than Colditz it was. I swear it was.' He frowned and rubbed his bald forehead. 'But I'd swear they weren't hiding in here before. Did I forget a door?'

Clipper grinned cheekily at him. 'It's all right, Mr Pratt. You didn't forget. I climbed in.'

He frowned harder. 'Can't be done.'

'Oh yes it can.' Looking very pleased with

herself, Clipper told him how she'd managed it. Exactly. In detail.

'*Caroline!*' Clipper's mother sat down suddenly on a chair. Mrs Gobbo heaved a massive arm round her shoulders and gave a comforting squeeze. Then she looked at the children and her face was thunderous. But all she said was, 'Get them ropes and things off you. Now.'

There was no need for her to say any more. The three of them would have stood out against policemen and teachers and even the Head Mister himself. But not against Mrs Gobbo. Now, meant now. Clipper began to fumble with her knots, and Spag started to mutter, 'Four, five, two, six? Six, five, four, two? Four, six, two, five?' Barny was rummaging frantically in his pockets, sweating in case he had lost his key.

'Bet Julius Caesar never had a mother,' he was mumbling. 'Bet Tarzan never had a mother. Bet Batman never had a mother. An' if they did, I bet they *gagged* them!'

His mum looked at him sharply. 'You ready, Barny Gobbo?'

'Yes Mum,' he said meekly.

'Well, you pick up them bits of paper off the floor, then. Who d'you think you are, scattering your rubbish all about?'

As he grabbed up the letters they'd written and shoved them in his pocket, she gave Clipper's mum another pat on the shoulder. Then she seized Barny's wrist and dragged him towards the door.

'Bye Spag. Bye Clipper,' he called defiantly. Might as well go out with a flourish. His mum was sure to erupt when she got him outside, on the stairs. His muscles tensed, ready for the outburst.

But – still nothing. Just the same ominous silence as she hustled him down the stairs, out of the building and along the road home, with her lips pressed tightly together.

It was a silence she did not break for nearly half an hour. She pushed Barny into the house, nodded her head to send him up to bed, and went in to have a word with his dad.

After a bit, Barny heard the front door slam. He knew what that meant. Dad had gone out. This was it. He snuggled as far down under the covers as he could, and closed his eyes tight, pretending to be asleep. But his heart was thundering as he listened to his mother's footsteps coming slowly up the stairs.

She walked into his bedroom and switched on the light.

'You can sit up for a start, my lad. Think I'm going to get taken in by your pretending? At my age?'

He dragged himself up, and sat blinking in the light, waiting for the shout.

Slowly, his mother lumbered across the room. She sat down jerkily on the edge of the bed and looked at him.

'Right now,' she said quietly. 'Tell us.'

He looked at her blankly. 'We told you. In the classroom. It's the school.'

She sighed. 'You *never* told me. Never tell me nothing. What was all that rubbish about bulldozers? Couldn't ask you in front of all them people, could I? Didn't want to make meself look an idiot. So tell. From the beginning.'

Barny took a deep breath and started at the beginning. With the letter he'd forgotten to give her. Then he went on about the bulldozers. About the painting and writing competitions and the flood in the bath. About Spag's advertisement, and Clipper in the ballet dress and the tomato ketchup. All about the purple bath and the bicycles. And then about the climbing into the school and the letters to the Queen and the Prime Minister and the television.

'And then you came,' he finished weakly, 'and that was the end of the sit-in and all the plans and – well – '

His mother looked at him. 'You got them letters?'

'In my trouser pocket. That's what you made me pick up off the floor.'

She reached over for his trousers and fished out the crumpled letters. Smoothing them out, she read them slowly, one by one. When she finished the last one, she crumpled them up together again and looked at him, shaking her huge head.

'Oh, you Gobbos,' she said. She was smiling, but her voice sounded almost ready to cry. 'All the same, you are. Just like your dad. He's always full of great schemes and big ideas. And what does it end up like? Eh?' She flourished a hand towards the window. 'Heaps of rubbish in the yard.'

Barny couldn't see what she was driving at. 'I like the heaps,' he said stoutly.

'Yes, well, you would, wouldn't you?' she said. 'Little Gobbo.' She levered herself up off the bed. 'Suppose you'd better get off to sleep then. Must be dog-tired.'

Barny looked up at her. Wasn't there going to be any shouting? None at all?

'Mum?'

'Yes?'

'I – sorry, Mum. It wasn't meant to be like that. We only meant – '

'Off to sleep now,' she said roughly. 'Don't want to hear another peep out of you. Had quite enough of you for one day.'

For a moment he saw her standing with her hand on the light switch, and then she flicked it and the room was pitch dark. Listening to her feet going downstairs again, he realised that she still had the three letters crumpled in her hand. Must be going to throw them in the bin. After all the effort he had put into doing his best writing for the Prime Minister. It wasn't fair. He shut his eyes and fell asleep instantly.

Downstairs, Mrs Gobbo spread out the three letters on the kitchen table and looked at them for a long time, shaking her head slightly. Then she found a clean sheet of paper and a pen, and began to write. After a few lines, she screwed the paper up, threw it on the floor and went to find another bit.

It took her a very long time, but at last she folded up her letter. She folded up, as well, the three letters that Barny, Spag and Clipper had written. Then she put all the pieces of paper into a brown envelope.

By the time Barny's father came home, the envelope was tucked behind the clock on the mantelpiece, waiting to be posted in the morning. It was addressed in big, straggly capital letters.

THE EDITOR,
THE SUNDAY NEWS,
FLEET STREET,
LONDON

8 · The Extraordinary Mr Reynolds

Clipper stood in the playground on Monday and stared miserably out over the town.

'That's it then,' she said. 'No more saving the school. No more ideas. Right?'

Tearing the old battered postcard into little pieces, she dropped them over the railings, like a shower of grubby confetti.

'Right,' said Spag. 'I don't want another weekend like last weekend.'

'Right, Gobbo?'

Barny grinned. His head felt completely empty, as if it would never have another idea in it if he lived to be a hundred. 'Right,' he said. 'It's over.'

And that's how it seemed. For weeks. And everything felt very flat. They'd grown so used to having secrets and working on the plan that now the days stretched out boringly, never-ending. Barny began to long for something else to start up, but every time he said 'Why don't we – ' or 'We could – ', Clipper knocked him down and sat on his head.

'Just you shut up, Gobbo. We've had enough trouble to last us till we're seventy.'

'Got to do something,' he muttered sulkily. 'Or we'll end up playing mums and dads with Elaine and Sharon.'

'If we do any more of your ideas,' Spag said firmly, 'We'll end up in prison.'

It looked as though nothing was going to happen, ever again.

But, one Thursday, they trooped into the classroom first thing in the morning and found Elaine bossily telling everyone, 'Full Assembly. Straight after register.'

'Not today,' Clipper said. 'It's Thursday. There's no assembly on Thursdays.'

'Mr Fox said. He just came in and said.' Elaine rolled her eyes with gruesome glee. 'There must be going to be a row. Someone's going to get into trouble.'

When they filed into the Hall and sat down, there was a strange man sitting on the platform next to the Head Mister. A huge man, with a scarlet shirt which made a bright blob of colour in the middle of the stage. His wide, broken-nosed face gazed inquisitively at the children marching into the Hall. Barny examined him from the top of his bushy, black hair to the muscular hands lying on his knees.

'He's going to give us free boxing lessons,' he mumbled out of the corner of his mouth.

Spag groaned softly, but Clipper said, 'Oh yummy. I wish they would.'

'Quietly, children.' The Head Mister frowned in their direction and then stood up as a signal to everyone that it was time to stop wriggling and listen to him.

As soon as they had settled, the Assembly began as usual, with hymns and prayers. Even though the hymns were good ones, the singing was only half strength. The children were too busy to sing. They were watching the stranger. He stood up very straight – he must have been nearly six foot six – towering over the Headmaster. And it was obvious that he was enjoying himself. He bellowed out all the hymns in a deep bass voice and after every prayer his booming 'Amen' drowned the usual school rumble.

As the last hymn finished, there was instant silence instead of the usual rustle of fidgeting. Everyone wanted to know why they had been called together, and who the stranger was.

'Now children, we have a very important visitor today.' The Headmaster gave the special smile he kept for visitors. 'This is Mr Geoff Reynolds. Some of you may have heard of him.' He paused hopefully, but all the faces gazing back at him were blank, and he hurried on.

'Mr Reynolds is a very well-known artist.'

'Blimey,' muttered Barny. He stared curiously

at the big man. He'd always thought that artists were little, weedy fellows.

'Some of you may remember,' the Headmaster went on, 'that earlier in the term every class did a painting for the *Sunday News* picture competition.'

Remember! Barny stared down at his feet and felt his face turn pink. Why did grown-ups always want you to remember the things you'd rather forget?

'Mr Reynolds,' for some reason the Headmaster sounded faintly surprised, 'has come to talk to us about the competition. I don't think I'll say any more than that. I'll let him explain. Mr Reynolds.'

There was a thin rattle of clapping round the Hall as the big man stood up and lumbered to the edge of the platform. He beamed down at the children.

'Smashing competition it was,' he said cheerfully. 'We had lots of pictures. Stacks and stacks of them. Pictures of jungles, processions, football matches, farms. All very pretty pictures, with the sky at the top and the ground at the bottom. Pretty as you like. Pretty, pretty, *pretty*!'

Quite unexpectedly, he pulled a disgusted face, and the children stared at him as if he were a snake charmer.

'Well, I ask you,' he said, 'did you ever see a pretty football match? Or a pretty farm, for that matter? Everyone knows farms are all mud and cows.'

Someone at the back giggled, and Mr Reynolds smiled.

'We had lots of pictures of *Our School* as well,' he said. 'And most of them were very, *very* pretty. Just like the football matches and the farms. In fact, it was hard to tell the difference sometimes.'

He snorted and waved an arm about. 'Pretty schools? Did you ever hear anything so stupid! Is this school pretty? Are you pretty? Of course you're not. You're a load of grubby, rude kids, aren't you?'

Most of the children laughed, but Elaine wriggled. 'I think he's a *horrid* man,' she whispered.

Mr Reynolds suddenly grinned at them all, as cheerfully as if he were Father Christmas. 'But it's all right. They weren't all like that.' He beamed

wider. 'We had one really smashing picture. Un-usual. Striking. Funny. Bet you never thought a picture could be funny, did you?'

All at once, he whirled round and strode to the side of the stage, where a big, blank piece of white card was propped against the wall.

'This is the picture. It's called *Our School*. It doesn't *look* like any school I've ever seen. But it *feels* like a school. It made me remember just what it was like to be at school. And because of that – ' he spun the picture round suddenly, as easily as if it were a playing card ' – because of that, it's won First Prize in our competition.'

'Gobbo!' Clipper was so startled that she spoke out loud. 'It's your bum!'

Everyone laughed. Nearly everyone. The children in the Hall fell about sideways, poking at each other and banging their feet. Mr Reynolds, on the platform, threw his head back and blared out a delighted roar of laughter. Even some of the teachers were smiling. The only two people in the Hall who were completely solemn were the Head Mister and Barny. The Headmaster was frowning as hard as he could without being rude to the visitor. Barny was just wishing that he could dis-appear through the floor.

'Told you it was funny,' Mr Reynolds said triumphantly. 'That's what schools are all about, isn't it? Gangs. Jokes. Soppy little girls chewing their plaits.'

'Lessons?' murmured Mr Fox, helpfully.

In front of Barny, Elaine snorted and pinched Clipper. It was the first time she had seen that drawing of herself, but she'd guessed who did it.

'Look here.' Mr Reynolds was prodding at the picture with his finger. 'This bloke on the roof. Eight feet tall and looking like Dracula. *Must* be the Headmaster.'

No one quite dared to laugh at that, but, surprisingly, the Head Mister gave a quick splutter of amusement as he stood up.

'I'm sure we'd all like to thank Mr Reynolds – ' he began.

'Hang on, old son.' Blandly, Mr Reynolds stuck up a hand. 'Haven't finished yet. Got something else very important to say.' He began to feel in the pockets of his tight trousers, wriggling about as he squeezed his fingers in. 'Know I've got the wretched thing somewhere.'

The children stared in silence, fascinated, waiting for the next surprise.

'Ah, here we are!' With a final wriggle, Mr Reynolds pulled some sheets of paper out of his pocket. 'You see, a funny thing happened when I went to tell the Editor of the *Sunday News* who'd won the competition. His secretary was there. And when I said "The Bennett Junior School", she jumped. Just like a rabbit.'

He jumped himself, to show them, and the stage shook.

'Then she said, "I've heard of that school," and she fished a letter out of the wastepaper basket.

That's what secretaries are for, you know. To throw letters away before anyone reads them.'

He spread out the top piece of paper in his hand. 'This was the letter she fished out.

Dear Sir,

They're going to close down my little boy's school, the Bennett Junior. All the children are very upset. Barny and his friends had a sit-in at the school and wrote to the Queen, but it wasn't any use. I think you could do something. Please will you help them?

Yours sincerely,
Mrs P. Gobbo.

P.S. I am sending you the letters they wrote, so you can see how upset they are.'

As he finished, the Hall was alive with whispers and giggles. But Mr Reynolds hadn't finished. He roared them into silence.

'Going to shut the school, are they? Well, we don't like that, me and the Editor of the *Sunday News*. This is a good school. There aren't many schools where the kids could turn out a picture like that.'

'I should hope not,' whispered Elaine primly. Clipper kicked her.

Mr Reynolds thumped the Headmaster's table with his fist, making the water jug rattle. 'Do you think we're going to let them close your school without a fight? Hey? The Editor told me to tell you all to read the *Sunday News* next Sunday. Front page. They'll put on a show for you. You'll see. That's all.' With a brisk, businesslike nod, he sat down again.

'Wow – ' Clipper started to say, but the Headmaster was already on his feet.

'I'm sure we'd all like to thank Mr Reynolds for his – his *surprising* news.' He floundered speechlessly for a moment. 'And – er – well, congratulations to Class Two for their prize-winning picture. Er – I think you'd all better go back to your classrooms now. Good morning, children.'

'Good morning, sir,' they chorused obediently.

By the time they got outside, Clipper was bouncing with glee. 'Gobbo!' She gave him a friendly punch that made him gasp. 'You did it! You actually did it! Like you said you would!'

'Ow! Clipper!' Barny wheezed. 'You got a licence for those fists? Anyway, what d'you mean? What've I done?'

'Saved the school, of course. Oh Gobbo, don't you see? The newspaper's going to make a fuss. It'll be all right!'

She danced off down the corridor. Barny looked at Spag. 'Gone off her head.'

'Oh, I dunno.' Spag suddenly gave a startling, enormous smile. 'At least there's going to be a gigantic row. They won't be able to shut the school down without anybody noticing much. Well done, Gobbo. You'll be a hero.'

'But I didn't – ' began Barny. Then he stopped. A broad, satisfied grin spread over his face. 'Of course,' he said casually, 'I always told you I was a genius, didn't I?'